Jake knew chemistry when he felt it

Taking on three kids and a single mom was bad enough, but that complication he did not need, unless it led only to a fast, uncomplicated affair. He was betting that a cheap affair was strictly off-limits with Lia.

So back off now, man. You don't need this.

Of course, that wasn't what his sister had been saying since Jake's return, with all her teasing about him finding a good woman and settling down. He'd claimed her brain had turned into romantic mush because of her wedding, but maybe she had a point.

He was thirty-nine and regimented in his ways. If he was ever going to give the marriage-and-family thing a legitimate shot, it should be soon. Never in his wildest dreams had he imagined hooking up with a woman with kids, especially when everything about them spelled trouble. Yet there was a certain efficiency about the situation that appealed, regardless of his ingrained habit of detachment.

One stop, no shopping.

A ready-made family.

Dear Reader,

There are times in a writer's life when fiction and reality intersect. I began the NORTH COUNTRY STORIES miniseries several years ago, using memories of my hometown as a basis for certain aspects of the fictional town of Alouette. Little did I know that I'd soon be moving back.

I purchased a house and acreage on the river that bisects the town. Directly across the bay from me is a magnificent wooded peninsula dotted with a dozen small stone houses—my original inspiration for the cottages that play a prominent role in both this book and *A Family Christmas* (Harlequin Superromance #1239). Although the real cottages are empty, I often gaze up at them as I swim the river, imagining them populated by my fictional couples. But the only character who has actually visited is the skunk!

Visit www.CarrieAlexander.com for more on the North Country books—both the real and the imaginary.

Warmly,

Carrie

A READY-MADE FAMILY

Carrie Alexander

HARLEQUIN®

TORONTO • NEW YORK • LONDON
AMSTERDAM • PARIS • SYDNEY • HAMBURG
STOCKHOLM • ATHENS • TOKYO • MILAN • MADRID
PRAGUE • WARSAW • BUDAPEST • AUCKLAND

ISBN-13: 978-0-373-71408-7
ISBN-10:   0-373-71408-4

A READY-MADE FAMILY

Printed in U.S.A.

ABOUT THE AUTHOR

Carrie Alexander began her writing career on a whim. Ten years later, she is the author of more than thirty books and a two-time RITA® Award finalist. The lifelong Michigander keeps busy working on her storybook cottage, where she paints anything that doesn't walk away—which explains the lime-green garbage can and floral mailbox.

Books by Carrie Alexander

HARLEQUIN SUPERROMANCE
1042—THE MAVERICK
1102—NORTH COUNTRY MAN*
1186—THREE LITTLE WORDS*
1239—A FAMILY CHRISTMAS*

*North Country Stories

Don't miss any of our special offers. Write to us at the following address for information on our newest releases.

Harlequin Reader Service
U.S.: 3010 Walden Ave., P.O. Box 1325, Buffalo, NY 14269
Canadian: P.O. Box 609, Fort Erie, Ont. L2A 5X3

To Cyndy and Crystalyn
When the going gets tough,
the tough get going in the Grudge

CHAPTER ONE

AFTER TWO DAYS ON THE road, getting lost, breaking down and spending her remaining cash at McDonald's to quiet the kids during the final stretch of their trip, was it possible that Lia Poguc's luck could get any worse?

Absolutely.

Her empty stomach gnawed as she watched the ambling approach of her second worst nightmare.

"Mom, you're crushing the map." Lia's ten-year-old son, Howie, tugged the gas station freebie out of her grip and refolded it with a pinched look of concentration. He'd been giving directions from the shotgun seat since they'd crossed the Mackinac bridge into the Upper Peninsula of Michigan, taking the job too seriously, as he did most tasks.

The cop circled Lia's idling car, slowing to study the back end. She didn't suppose he was admiring the vintage rust on the 1980 Impala they called "the Grudge" or the buckety-buck of a motor misfiring on its ancient pistons. Surreptitiously she rubbed her sweaty palms on her knee-length denim shorts, trying to keep the kids from seeing her nervousness. Was the uniform cop writing down her license plate number? What if it had already shown up on some sort of Most Wanted list?

That's not possible. Larry doesn't know we're gone—yet.

"Mom?" warbled Sam from the backseat as her eyes followed the police officer's circuit. Because she knew what was at stake, she'd forgotten to act jaded. Her mascara-thickened lashes had widened in alarm.

"Everything's all right." Lia had repeated some variation of the phrase for the past few days. Longer, actually, but she didn't want to go there right now. She said it so often that the words came out even when it was clear that everything was wrong.

Everything except the most important fact: they were free.

Maybe not for long.

The cop tapped on her window.

She exhaled. "Don't talk," she told her kids before rolling down the glass. The Grudge had crank windows. For once, she was glad. She had something to do to distract herself from the tight ache wanting to burst out of her chest.

The officer tipped back his cap and peered into the car, taking in the jumble of discarded clothing, children's toys and fast-food trash that had accumulated during the long drive north. "Everybody okay in there?"

"Yes, sir." *Don't volunteer information.*

"Ya, well." He smiled, clearly a small-town cop because he didn't flinch when Lia reached down beside her, toward the seat. He was looking at the map clenched in her son's lap. "Gotchyerselves lost, eh?"

She sucked on the straw of Howie's Coke to wet her dry mouth. "Sort of."

"Whatcha looking for?" The neighborly cop leaned an arm on her car door. "I can give you directions to anyplace in the whole U.P."

He was young, blond and rather goofy-looking with a Barney Fife face that was all nose and Adam's apple with not much chin in between. His accent was even heavier than her old friend Rose Robbin's—"ya" for "yeah" and "da" for "the."

Nothing threatening about him, but Lia didn't relax. Fugitives couldn't afford to let down their guard.

"Thanks, but we'll be fine." She didn't want him to know where she was headed. If Alouette was as small as Rose had said—and it certainly appeared to be from their hillside vantage point—he'd find out soon enough. Lia didn't see any need for currying interest, even friendly interest. Not from any of the locals. After the first curiosity had passed, she hoped to knit her family into the fabric of small-town life so well that no one ever noticed them again.

Howie shoved his glasses up his snub nose. "This map doesn't show Black—"

Lia gave him a look so fierce his voice froze mid-stream.

The cop tilted his head. "Sounds to me like you're lost."

The car's engine rattled ominously. Lia hadn't dared shut it down while they'd searched the map. If she didn't put the Grudge into gear soon, it might give out again.

She thrust the soft drink at her son. "We were just taking a breather," she said to the cop in a fake cheery tone, the one she'd used too often with her children the past several years. Kristen Rose, her four-year-old, was the only one who still fell for it. "We'll be on our way now."

The officer tilted his head to the right, checking out the backseat. Lia felt Sam's clogs press into her spine through the car seat. Her teenage daughter's long, skinny legs were doubled over and drawn up to her sulky face. She glared raccoon eyes at the officer over her kneecaps, as if daring him to question her.

Smile, dammit, Lia said silently in the rearview mirror. *Just this once.*

"I'm Deputy Corcoran." He looked at Lia expectantly.

Lia met Sam's accusing eyes in the mirror, then looked away. "Lia Howard," she said almost too loudly. She wasn't lying, not really. She'd been Lia Howard for the first seventeen years of her life. "And these are my kids." She wasn't going to give their names unless she had to.

Officer Corcoran tipped his hat. "Pleased to meetcha."

Lia made a polite sound.

In the rear seat, Kristen stirred. The drive through twenty miles of backcountry forest had been so boring that she'd nodded off with a French fry clutched in her small fist. "Mommy? Are we there yet?"

"Not yet," Lia said before Howie could chime in that, yes, they'd finally reached their destination, even if they couldn't find Blackbear Road on the state map.

"How come we stopped? Is the Grudge broked again?"

"No, honey." Lia's eyes darted toward the officer's face. Kristen didn't completely understand the necessity of keeping quiet, especially around strangers. But she was learning. And that had taken another small chip out of Lia's worn-down heart. "We'll be there soon."

"Not with this car," the cop said. "The motor doesn't sound too good."

"I know. That's why we call it the Grudge." At his mystified look, she explained, "It's from a horror movie. My daughter came up with the name. Because of the loud grinding sound the car makes when it revs up."

"I getcha, I guess. I'm darn surprised you made it to town. The 525 might not seem like a steep road, but it's got a long, gradual incline."

"Luckily it's all downhill from here." Lia forced a chuckle as she gave a wave out the front window at the descent into the town proper.

They were perched on a hillside overlooking Alouette. The sight was a pretty one, if Lia had been in any shape to appreciate it. Interspersed among an abundance of summery green trees were the shingle roofs, cream brick and red sandstone of the quaint little town. Beyond, the blue water of Lake Superior stretched as far as the eye could see. A lighthouse perched at the tip of a finger peninsula pointing into the bay. Gulls circled bobbing boats in the small marina.

Officer Corcoran had straightened to take in the view, but he ducked back down to address her. "Didja know you have a busted taillight?"

"Oh." She knew. But a working taillight was less crucial than replacing spark plugs and a fried fan belt—the emergency repair that had kept them stranded overnight in the middle of nowhere in a town called Christmas. "I'll get it fixed as soon as I can," she promised, which was honest enough considering *soon* was an adaptable word.

For how many years had she planned to leave her husband "soon"? After the divorce had gone through despite Larry's attempts to block it, she'd learned a new definition of the word. *Soon* he'll stop trying to hurt us. *Soon* the courts will understand. *Soon* we'll get away.

"I shouldn't let you go without a ticket, but…" The cop disappeared from her window to wave at a pickup truck that rattled by on the bumpy blacktop road. It shed flecks of rust like a dog shaking fleas. The young officer grinned. "See there? I gotta admit our department's not a stickler when it comes to ticketing unroadworthy vehicles." He squared his shoulders. "But it's important to keep your family's safety in mind."

Lia swallowed. He had no idea. "I do, sir. Always."

The young officer stepped back. "You be sure to get the vehicle fixed, ma'am. I don't want to see it on the road again in this condition."

"You won't." Lia let herself hope that she'd finally caught a break. "We don't have far to go," she added. "We'll be there long before dark." Kristen was fussing in the backseat, and Sam—bless her—passed over her precious iPod to keep her sister occupied.

"All right, then." Officer Corcoran moved away from the car. "Make sure to watch your brakes on this hill. Speed limit's twenty-five in town." He squinted. "Are you positive you don't want directions?"

"No, thanks." Lia knew where she was going.

Anywhere that her ex-husband Larry Pogue was not.

ALOUETTE WASN'T LARGE enough to be lost in for very long. After creeping down the hill and through the handful of streets that made up the downtown area, they drove around until they found Blackbear Road on the northern side of town. Lia's memory of the location of their destination was sketchy, pulled from years-old conversations with Rose Robbin about her hometown.

Rose would have supplied better directions if she'd known they were coming, but Lia hadn't told her. In fact, they hadn't talked in nearly a month, when Rose had called to tell Lia she was getting married. Because her friend deserved uncomplicated happiness, Lia had oohed and aahed and kept her escalating troubles to herself.

Now she had no choice. She was desperate for a safe haven.

"This is it, Mom." Howie stuck his head out the window to read the peeling board sign obscured by a thicket of underbrush. "Maxine's Cottages."

Relaxing her shoulders for the first time in an hour, Lia turned the car onto a twisting dirt-and-pebble road. Towering pines threw shadows across the Impala's long hood. Hidden among the trees were small stone cottages, just as Rose had described. They seemed a natural part of the landscape. Their slanted roofs were thick with pine needles, the stone walls covered in moss, lichen and overgrown vines.

The road widened into a clearing near the largest structure, the central home with a plaque that denoted the office. A big black pickup truck was parked at a careless angle, taking up most of the space. Lia pulled in next to it and shut off the engine, which reluctantly gave up the ghost. Buckety-buck. Buck. Buck. The tailpipe popped. Exhaust smoke drifted by her open window, temporarily masking the fresh piney smell of the woods.

Lia breathed deeply anyway. They'd made it. Thank God.

"We're here," she announced.

The children stared in total silence.

"It's not so bad."

A protest burst from Sam. "We can't stay here! It's abandoned."

"It's not abandoned." But the only signs of occupancy were the truck, limp curtains that fluttered in an open window of the stone house and a fishing pole and a rake leaning against a rail by the front door.

"Can we get out?" Howie asked.

"I'm not," Sam said, crossing her arms across her chest and sliding even lower in the seat until only the blue-tipped spikes of her bangs showed. "I want to go home."

"Then you'll have to push the Grudge, because its engine won't make the return trip." Lia put on her cheery voice as she reached for the door handle. "Let's go see if anyone's home. Rose said there's a river nearby. Can you hear it?"

"I do." Howie's door creaked as he pushed it open. He was small for his age, still a little boy despite the anxious personality and smarts that made him seem older than his years. One of Lia's greatest wishes was to see Howie relax. To run and play, to learn how to be a boy without responsibility.

He looked eagerly at Lia across the hood, light reflecting off his glasses.

She stretched the kinks from her back. "All right. Go and explore." She held back warnings about snakes and poison ivy and deep water. Howie didn't have to be told. His caution was even stronger than his curiosity.

"Come on, Krissy, baby." Lia took her youngest child's hand as the girl slid out of the back seat. Sticky. Kristen's lips were stained with orange soda pop. Lia grabbed a packet of wet wipes from the glove compartment and squatted to apply one to her daughter's hands and face. Kristen blinked sleepy eyes as she looked up at the trees and sky. She was a slow riser.

Lia rubbed at Kristen's small, plump mouth until only a faint orange shadow remained. She smoothed the girl's rumpled T-shirt. "Want to knock on the front door for me?"

Kristen stared at the gloomy stone house. "Who lives there?"

"Rose Robbin does." Or did. "Her mother, too. You probably can't remember Rose—the dark-haired lady who was our neighbor? She used to babysit you when you were just a tiny little baby."

"Uh-uh."

"She babysat all of you kids." Surly Rose had been a loner who'd gradually warmed up to the Pogues. She'd become Lia's friend and confidante, the only person she could rely on. But when Rose's father had died several years ago, she'd gone home to Alouette in Michigan's U.P.—Upper Peninsula. They'd lost contact for a long while, until Rose had mailed a Christmas card the past December. Since then, they'd written and called a number of times. When Rose had first learned that Larry was still causing trouble, she'd offered Lia help any time she needed it.

Misgivings nibbled at Lia's conscience. At the moment of crisis, with Larry threatening to sue her for custody of the children and even hinting that he'd snatch them away if he had to, she'd latched on to Rose's offer as her only option. She and the kids had needed to disappear. According to Rose, Alouette was the type of place where you could do that.

Not the end of the Earth, the welcome sign had read on the way into town, *but we can see it from here.*

As much as Lia appreciated the isolation, she hadn't expected to feel quite so stranded and alone. Maybe she'd thought Rose would greet them with an apple pie. Even though she had no idea they were coming.

Lia tried the cheery voice on herself. *Won't Rose be surprised that we've traveled hundreds of miles to land on her doorstep?*

"Hey, Mom!" Howie called from the trees. "There's more little houses over here." He'd found a path. Through the thick stand of evergreens, Lia caught glimpses of him running from cottage to cottage. "Four on this side."

Kristen looked up at Lia, her eyes glistening. "I don't wanna live here, Mommy."

Lia stroked Kristen's hair. Her girl was usually

more adventurous. The completely unfamiliar landscape must have thrown her off-kilter. "Let's wait and
see how we like it."

"See?" Sam said peevishly from her slumped position inside the car. "Nobody wants to stay here."

Lia took Kristen's hand. "Would you like to join us,
Sam?"

A huffy exhale came from the back seat. "Hell no."

Lia's mouth tightened. Samantha was fourteen and
getting more rebellious every day. Their neighborhood
in Cadillac hadn't been the greatest, and if they'd come
north for no other reason, Lia was relieved to get Sam
away from the crowd of teenagers she'd taken up with
back home. Sam might actually be correct about one
of her litany of complaints—there'd be nothing to do
in a small town like Alouette. At least nothing that her
mother wouldn't know about.

Lia was counting on that. She wanted her bright,
lively daughter back—or some teenage semblance,
anyway.

She shrugged. "Suit yourself, Sam." Maybe she was
copping out on her responsibilities as a mother, but
now wasn't the time to engage her eldest in a battle
over language and attitude. Sam could sit in the car and
stew. If they stayed in Alouette, she'd adjust to the
idea. She'd adjusted to worse.

The thought was little comfort.

"Howie?" Lia finger-combed her own hair as she
and Kristen walked to the front door of the stone house.

She felt rumpled and creased, like a grocery bag that had been used too many times.

His voice drifted from the trees. "Yeah, Mom."

"Just checking."

"I'm over here. I found mushrooms."

"Don't eat them. And don't wander off."

There were three steps up to the front entry, a weather-beaten plank door with a placard that read Office. No doorbell, except for an old-fashioned dinner bell that hung from a rusty bracket. Lia knocked.

And waited.

She knocked again, looking around the run-down property. The cottages were placed in random order, tucked here and there in groves of pines, maples and birches. Chickadees and nuthatches hopped among the pinecones that littered the ground. Sam watched owlishly over the edge of the car seat, showing the whites of her eyes. Still no answer.

"Look, Mommy." Kristen pointed to the bell suspended beside the door. "Can I ring it?"

"I guess so." Lia lifted the girl, showing her how to tug on the short rope attached to the gong.

The sturdy metal bell rang out deep and loud. Kristen laughed at the sound and reached out again, but Lia stopped her. "Enough. If anyone's home, they ought to have heard that."

Kristen slid down. "Can I go with Howie?"

"All right." Lia stepped away from the door and aimed her daughter toward the path through the overhanging trees. Kristen took off like a shot, much braver now that she was fully awake. Lia smiled at the enthusiasm, wishing *her* courage was as easily reinstated. "Howie, please watch out for Kristen."

Lia waited until she heard their voices before giving in to her own curiosity. With one more glance at the Grudge, she walked around to the back of the house. Sam's head had sunk below window level.

Lia inhaled. The sharp, spicy scent of pines filled her lungs. God, the air was fresh here. The house had no lush suburban lawn, only ragged patches of grass poking out from beneath a thick blanket of coppery pine needles. Inside a sagging wire fence, a patch had been cleared for a garden, the rich earth freshly overturned and planted with seedlings. The level area near the house became a slope that steepened down to a reedy riverbank.

Lia shielded her eyes. The dark river swirled and eddied, rushing white where submerged rocks had been worn silky and smooth by the constant flow. Cattails nodded in the breeze.

Despite the shabbiness, the setting was idyllic. A piece of paradise. Lia began to understand why Rose had returned despite her less-than-idyllic childhood. If Lia had grown up in a place like this, she might not have been in such a rush to leave home that she'd latched on to her first real boyfriend and mistaken his intense feelings for true, deep love.

Rose had told her own tale, those long evenings

when they'd sat out on the small lawn of their apartment building, sharing a pack of cigarettes and the sad tales of their lives while the kids played Kick the Can. According to her, paradise wasn't always what it was cracked up to be. But Rose had found a happy ending here all the same.

A happy ending was more than Lia dared to dream of. Even though a piece of paradise might be nice, she'd gladly settle for simple peace.

She sighed, rubbing her forehead. Had she made a mistake becoming a fugitive instead of trying to work things out within the law, even if that had already taken years and every cent she earned? It seemed so now, when she was tired and broke, but in her gut she knew that fleeing was the only way she and the kids had a chance at a normal life. If they'd stayed, Larry would have never let up.

Lia turned back to the house. She'd suspected Rose might be gone, but what had happened to her mother? And there'd been a brother, too, back from the Army. Or maybe it was the one who'd been in prison.

At the window, she made a visor with her hands to peer inside. No one in sight, but there was a table stacked high with gift boxes that probably contained enough small kitchen appliances to stock a department store.

She groaned. She should have brought a present. But what? A used coffeemaker? A blender that could only puree on low?

Dismayed with herself, Lia reached inside her shirt to rescue a fallen bra strap that was held together by a pin. She'd once been a genuinely cheerful girl—a cheerleader, even—with shiny blond hair and a set of days-of-the-week underpants. The most important appliance in her life had been her curling iron. So how had her life turned into a wreckage of broken-down motors and tatty undergarments?

She was startled by a deep male voice. "Find anything good in there?"

Her fingers clenched on the bra strap. *A deflated but still serviceable pair of 34Cs* was the answer that popped into her mind before she realized the man was referring to her spying through the window.

"I was looking for Rose." She withdrew her hand from her shirt and tucked it in the pocket of her shorts. "Rose Robbin? Am I in the right place?"

The man gave her a once-over, his blunt, stony face betraying none of his thoughts. He was tall and rawboned, thick with muscles in the way of a hard worker who'd developed an iron-hard physique with years of physical labor. He wore heavy boots and khaki cargo pants despite the warm weather. The open collar and cuffs of his shirt displayed a strong neck and massive forearms inscribed from wrist to elbow with complicated tattoos. There was something not quite civilized about him.

Lia's heart beat a little faster. Rose's brother, she presumed, but was it the ex-con or the military man?

What direction had he come from? And where were her kids?

She sidled over a couple of steps. "I didn't mean to snoop. Well, yes, I suppose I did, since I was snooping. But I didn't mean to be rude. I wondered where everyone had gone, that's all. The house seemed deserted. I, um, that is, we—me and my kids—came for the wedding."

"You're late."

"I know. My car broke down."

"The wedding was yesterday."

"I'm sorry we missed it."

He scanned her again, apparently not happy with what he saw, because he scowled, the color in his tanned face getting even darker. "Rose is on her honeymoon."

"Oh." The dregs of Lia's last hope leaked out of her. She realized what a bind she'd put herself in. No cash, nowhere to stay. Only a small amount of wiggle room remained on her credit card. "I figured it was something like that. But we had a long drive and it was too late to turn back." She crossed her fingers inside her pockets. "So we came anyway."

"How many is we?"

"I have three children. Oh—I didn't introduce myself." But then, neither had he. She didn't stick out her hand. He looked as if he might bite it. "I'm Lia Howard."

"Jake Robbin." He didn't budge an inch.

"You're Rose's oldest brother. She's mentioned me?"

"No, ma'am."

"She invited me to the wedding a while back. I told her then I couldn't make it, only I changed my mind at the last minute. We were neighbors several years ago." She was babbling.

His nod was neither an acknowledgment nor an agreement. "Too bad you missed her."

"Yes, too bad," she said. The sympathy on his face was underwhelming. "We'll move on, of course." She gritted her teeth so the desperation wouldn't show. "We wouldn't want to put you out." Not that he'd offered. "My kids can be quite a handful." She gestured toward the front yard, embarrassed to see Kristen's stretchy pink-lace-and-glitter ponytail holder around her wrist like a bracelet. "They're over there—"

On cue, Kristen came chugging around the side of the house with her hands flapping. "Mom! Mom! Howie found a skunk!" She barreled into Lia's legs. "It's gonna bite him."

Lia winced. "Do skunks bite?" she asked Jake. Before he had time to answer, she hurried off the way Kristen had come.

Jake loped beside her, ducking tree branches because he was so tall. "Probably not. Unless it's rabid." He put out his arm, slowing her down as they reached the path to the cottages. "Don't run. Sudden movement will scare it, and—believe me—you don't want that to happen."

Kristen had caught up to them. She stared up at

Jake with a finger in her mouth. She took it out. "What happens if we scare the skunk?"

Jake's firm lips twitched. He squeezed two fingers on the tip of his nose and said, "Pew."

Kristen giggled, copying the gesture. "Pew!"

Lia blinked. "Did you say *pew?*"

"Haven't you ever smelled skunk?"

"Of course. I was— Never mind." She was amused by the word, that was all. Maybe he wasn't a hard case all the way through. "Let's rescue Howie before he's sprayed."

"I'll go," Jake said. "You keep the little girl out of range."

Lia almost laughed at the way Kristen's upper body swayed forward. Her lower lip protruded. "I'm not a little girl. My name is Kristen Rose."

Jake was moving silently along the path, but he stopped to look back at them. "Kristen Rose, huh? Pretty name." He shot a look at Lia. "After my sister?"

She nodded. "I told you we were friends." When she'd gone into labor, Rose had stayed home from work to look after Sam and Howie while Lia delivered the new baby. During the especially tough times immediately after her divorce, Lia had learned to treasure such small acts of kindness.

Howie's voice floated from the trees. "Mo-om?"

"Don't move, Howie," she called. "Stay there and tell us where you are."

"I'm sitting on the step of one of the little houses."

Lia crept after Jake, trying to keep Kristen behind her. They moved past the first two cottages and came to the third, where Howie perched on the doorstep, his arms and legs pulled close to his skinny body. A skunk sniffed through the long grass at the cottage's foundation, barely two feet away from the boy. Its silky tail swept the ground. A faint but distinctly bitter aroma scented the air.

Jake stopped. He rested his hands on his hips, as casual as if they were on a Sunday afternoon stroll. "Howie? Don't move, okay?" He spoke in a soft, even voice. "I'm Jake. I live here and I've seen this skunk before. Don't worry. He'll go on his way in a minute."

The creature lifted its head. A moist black nose twitched in Howie's direction.

He cringed. Behind the glasses, his eyes were big and scared. "It's gonna spray me," he whispered in a quavery high pitch.

Jake moved closer. He squatted. "No, see how his tail is down? The skunk's curious about you, but he's not afraid. He uses his sense of smell and hearing because he can't see very well. He needs glasses like yours."

Lia chuckled to ease Howie's fear, but he didn't seem to be persuaded that this was a laughing matter. "You're sure he won't spray me?"

"Yep," Jake said. "Only if he thinks you're going to hurt him."

Howie's chest hitched. Lia's heart melted at how

brave he was trying to be. "Uh-huh. I kn-know that. I read about skunks in my science and nature book."

"What else did you read?"

Howie watched warily as the skunk lowered its head and the tail came up slightly. "I read—I read—" He closed his eyes. "Skunks are mammals. And they're nocturnal."

"What does that mean?" Jake asked gently.

Howie squinched his nose. "They sleep in the day. So how come—" He gasped as the skunk turned toward him.

"Slide over," Jake directed. "Slowly."

Howie inched sideways until he sat at the very corner of the step. The skunk ambled out of the grass, toward the path blocked by Jake.

He kept his eyes on Howie. "Now you can stand. Do it slowly. That's right. The skunk's okay, just going for a stroll. He's not even looking at you."

Lia stooped to see past the obscuring evergreens. Jake was right. The animal was ignoring Howie because it was waddling toward Jake. She held her breath.

Jake didn't move. His voice remained calm. "Keep going, Howie. Walk past me toward your mom. You'll be fine."

Jake waited until Howie had crept by, then rose slowly off his heels, keeping himself between the boy and the skunk. His boots scuffed the ground as he edged backward, widening the distance.

Lia caught Howie's eye. She gave him an encouraging smile. He grinned sheepishly, hitching his thumbs in his belt loops and swaggering just a little, as if he'd never been frightened in the first place.

Kristen pushed against Lia's leg. "Can I pet the skunk?" she whispered.

"That's not a good idea with an untamed animal." Lia reached down and swung Kristen up in her arms in case the girl got it into her head to run toward the small striped creature.

"But it's pretty."

"We're in the wild, honey. It's not like a petting zoo." Lia turned back in the direction of the car, keeping her eye on Howie to be sure he was following. But he'd stopped, too busy looking up at Jake with awe to worry about escaping from the skunk.

Which was when disaster struck.

"Hey, guys!" Sam's shout was impatient. The sudden blare of the car horn shattered the silence as she punched it over and over again.

"Sam!" Lia shrieked. "Stop it!"

Too late.

The skunk's tail had shot straight up. Jake let out a shout and sprang backward, his arms pinwheeling as an overwhelmingly putrid, eye-watering stench coated the air.

CHAPTER TWO

JAKE PLUNGED INTO THE cold water of the river, a bar of soap in hand. His eyes and nose stung with the acrid stench that rose off his body. He dived for relief, surfacing quickly as he remembered that he wasn't alone.

The boy stood shivering at the shore, stripped to shorts and T-shirt. He'd hadn't received the full brunt of spray like Jake, but had insisted that he needed to bathe in the river, too, once he'd seen that was what Jake intended. The kid's mother had been hesitant, staring up at Jake with big, blue, scaredy-cat eyes. And sure enough, he could see her through the trees at the top of the hill, wringing her hands as she watched over them.

"Jump in," Jake said.

Howie waded deeper. "How come it's so cold?"

"It's a fast, deep river. It's always cold, even in July." Jake began scrubbing with the soap. Little good that would do except maybe take the edge off. The skunk smell was so strong he could taste it.

The boy's eyes were watering. He squeezed his shoulders into his neck and took another wobbly step deeper into the swirling water.

His timidity made Jake impatient. "C'mon. Get dunked." He thought of his father, Black Jack, roaring with laughter as he tossed a five-year-old Jake and his even younger brother into the deep water although they could barely dog-paddle at the time. *Your mother doesn't want you drowning,* he'd said. *Be men, not pansies. Swim!*

Jake had swum. He couldn't remember if he'd been scared like Howie, but he supposed that was possible.

"Stop thinking about it. Jump."

The boy sucked in a breath and surged forward, sputtering and flailing as the current swept him toward Jake. He paddled strenuously, holding his head high out of the water like a nervous dog. Up on the hill, the woman started down, then stopped as Jake reached out and plucked her son from the water, setting him upright near a heap of rocks that protruded into the river.

"Good man." Jake passed the bar. "Soap up."

Without his glasses, Howie looked owlishly at bare-chested Jake, then stripped off his own shirt, exposing a skinny white torso. He rubbed himself into a froth and they plunged into the deep water again to rinse themselves clean. The scent of skunk was not so easily defeated.

Jake urged Howie out of the water. He collected their discarded clothing into one reeking armful.

The boy fumbled for the glasses he'd tucked in his shoe. He put them on and studied Jake's tattoos with fascination. After a minute, the corners of his mouth jerked into a tight little smile. "Hey, Jake. You still stink."

"So do you." Jake squeezed water from his boxer shorts, then chafed his arms and legs. "And you look like a drowned cat."

"My mom's gonna be mad."

Jake didn't think so. She seemed more like the fussbudget type. "Not your fault the skunk found you."

"I was exploring in the forest."

"So you're saying that it was you who found the skunk?"

"Sort of. I think it followed me." The shivering boy looked up with a worried face. "I'm sorry you got sprayed."

Jake clapped him on the shoulder. "Not the first time. No big deal."

"But you really stink. Worse'n me."

"It'll wear off." Jake shoved his feet into his boots and started up the slope to the house. "C'mon. Your mom will have dry clothes for you."

She did. Towels, too, unfamiliar to Jake. "Yours?" he said, taking the one she offered—a faded beach towel printed with some kind of cartoon character.

"I had them in the car." She was vigorously rubbing down her son, and the poor kid stood there and took it, jiggling like a bobblehead doll.

"Uh, thanks, but I'm liable to ruin it." Jake tried to hand back the towel. "According to Howie, I still stink."

"Yeah, you do." She screwed up her face. "But go ahead and use the towel anyway. It's an old one." Her glance bounced off him. "And you look pretty cold."

Jake had dropped the pile of ruined clothes. He stood before her in nothing but unlaced boots, soaked cotton shorts, tattoos and dog tags. He was probably showing a little too much of the raw package down below. While he had no modesty left after decades as an Army Ranger, she obviously wasn't as easygoing.

He dried himself, then wrapped the towel around his hips. He watched her help Howie step into a pair of jeans and asked, "What was your name again?" even though he remembered she was Leah…something.

She looked up from a kneel. "Lia Po—Howard. Lia Howard."

"Huh." He looked at the boy. "So you're Howie Howard?"

Howie opened his mouth. Lia thrust a polo shirt down over his head. "Howie's a nickname."

Her daughters came around the corner of the house, holding hands. They stared at Jake.

He eyed them. The little girl was a cutie. The teenager clearly had an attitude, considering the way she thrust her chin and glowered at him, the sun glinting off the silver stud pierced beneath her lower lip.

She made a choking sound and pressed the back of her hand to her nose. Black polish was chipping off her nails. Around one thin wrist was a wide leather band, heavy chain link on the other. "That smell. I can't stand it."

Lia frowned. "Sam, don't be rude."

"But, Mom, he reeks." The girl gagged, then gagged again with her hand pressed over her mouth. "Gross. It's making me sick." She turned and ran off. They heard the car door slam.

"That was Sam," Lia said. "Samantha. She's fourteen with a vengeance."

"Needs a paddling."

Lia's words popped like mortar fire. "I don't hit my kids. Violence solves nothing."

Jake shrugged. "That depends on the situation."

"You're the soldier, then."

"The soldier?"

"Rose told me. One brother in the Army, one brother…" She trailed off as if embarrassed.

Jake gave her a look. "In the big house."

"Where's the big house?" the little girl asked. She pointed. "That one?"

"A different kind of house, honey."

"Prison," Howie said. He was looking at Jake with the same rounded eyes his mother used. "Were you in combat?"

"Yeah."

"Are you going back?"

"I'm retired now."

Howie squinted. "You don't look that old."

"I'm thirty-nine. Old enough to retire from the Army. I enlisted when I was eighteen."

"My mom got married when she was seventeen."

"Oh?" Jake watched the emotion that crossed Lia's face before she felt his interest and made herself go blank. He directed his comment at her. "You went through a different kind of combat, huh?"

She let out a little snort. "You could say that."

"We're divorced from Daddy," piped up Kristen Rose.

Lia clenched her hands. "I'm divorced, not you kids."

"Then when can we see Daddy again?"

"I don't know." Lia evaded Jake's curiosity by reaching for the discarded clothing. She got one whiff and dropped the garments. "The smell is really bad, even on Howie. We're going to have to do something about it or we won't be allowed into a motel."

The boy cocked his head. "A motel? But—"

"Hush, Howie. We're going to a motel." Lia sent a distracted but apologetic smile at Jake. "We've caused enough trouble for Mr. Robbin."

Jake knew that he ought to keep his mouth shut and let them leave. He wanted them to go. He had big plans for the place and he surely didn't want to work around the distraction of three kids and a needy woman. Only the thought of Rose scolding him for being a bad host in her stead made him speak up. "You're going to run off and leave me stinking like this?"

Lia showed surprise. "Well, of course I'd like to help, but I don't know what I can—"

"I know," Howie said. "We have to take baths in tomato juice."

"Sounds kind of icky, but if you want to try it…" Lia looked at Jake. "Do you have any tomato juice?"

He thought of the nearly bare cupboards and fridge. Chili and beans, a few cans of tuna. Beer, mustard, ketchup. "I sincerely doubt it."

"I, um, I guess I could go to the store."

Jake had heard the racket when they drove up. That car shouldn't go anywhere until he'd taken a look at the engine and the brakes. "You can take my truck."

Lia hesitated, looking worried. "All right." She reached for her daughter's hand, protective as a mama bear. "We'll all go to the store for tomato juice."

"I'm staying here with Jake," Howie announced.

"Oh, no, you're not."

Jake tightened his jaw and kept silent. For about two seconds. Then he glanced at Howie's hopeful face. "It's okay. He can stay."

The boy beamed.

Shit, Jake thought, but mostly out of habit. "He reeks too much to go in my truck."

Howie sniffed himself. His narrow chest expanded. "Yeah, I reek."

Lia aimed the big blues at Jake. "Are you sure?"

He scowled, not used to being questioned. "I know my own mind."

"Lucky you."

Lucky? "And I don't say what I don't mean."

Her stare became skeptical. "That must be interesting."

"Not so much. I also know when to keep my mouth shut."

"Huh. There's a talent."

She sounded weary, maybe a little wistful. Jake's antennae went up, before he reminded himself that she was a mom who'd been on a road trip with a broken-down car and three children who weren't shy about their opinions.

She looked the worse for the wear. Her pale blond hair was caught up at the back of her head with straggly wisps hanging loose. A wayward bra strap peeked out from the sleeveless pink blouse that was wrinkled and untucked from a pair of baggy shorts. Nice legs. But no tan. White socks sagged at her ankles. Her five-dollar-bin tennis shoes were scuffed and fraying at the pinkie toes. Around one wrist was a rubber band, a grimy braided string knotted into place and a stretchy bracelet made of pink sparkly frills and doodads.

Jake's eyes went back up. Lia's face was pretty enough when she wasn't looking hassled or worried, but she wasn't his type. Not that he actually had a type except for knowing from the age of sixteen what he didn't need: women who clung, women who whined, women with great expectations.

Since he'd been back in Alouette and seen tough little Wild Rose so happy and content with her fiancé, there'd grown a few doubts in Jake's mind that maybe the Robbin siblings weren't destined to be loners after all. He'd even experienced a rare loneliness, on his own, without his squadron, without orders, without a firm plan for the future. Rose had been thrilled to have him back—hell, she'd hugged him so hard he'd had bruises the next day—but she'd also been busy with her new family and wedding plans. When the twittering bridesmaids had descended, Jake had made himself scarce.

He ran a hand through his damp hair, already grown out some from its Army-issue zip cut. Rose would read him the riot act if he didn't offer her friend a place to stay. But she was on her honeymoon for a week or so, which would leave him with too many days of goggle-eyed attitude, worship and questions from the Howard children. What he'd get from Lia was anyone's guess.

Jake kept his mouth shut, not so sure he wanted to find out.

Lia had taken another sniff of Howie. "It's not that bad. You should come along so we don't impose on Mr. Robbin more than we already have."

Howie's face fell. "But I stink."

She gave him a stern look. "Not that bad. You're mostly smelling Mr. Robbin."

Howie looked at Jake, hoping for help.

He shrugged. If Lia was going to be stubborn, he wouldn't insist.

Now she was looking doubtfully at his heavy-duty pickup truck, a GMC Sierra, parked in front of the main house. "You know how to drive a stick?" he asked and tossed her the keys that had been in his pocket when he'd gotten skunked.

She caught them, her expression remaining hesitant even when she nodded. "I can drive a stick. But I need— I need—" Now she was pained. "Money," she finally blurted. Her face went red. "For the tomato juice. I'll have to get a lot of the large-size cans to make a bath for…" Her gaze skipped across his chest before pinning itself on his left ear while she said in a rush, "A big man like you."

"No problem. My wallet's inside. In fact, if you don't mind, you can pick up a few groceries for me while you're at it." The thought at the back of his mind was that the food was actually for them, but if she was broke, he didn't want her to feel like a charity case. "Milk, bread, eggs, fruit, hamburger—that kind of stuff. Okay?"

"Okay." She let out a breath of relief. "I'm happy to help. I owe you for taking one for my son."

"Forget it." Jake suppressed the urge to give her one more lingering look. He went inside instead. If he stomped more than usual, it was only because that with all of her darting glances, she'd made him aware of how odd he must look wearing a towel and combat boots.

"I DON'T WANT TO STAY there." Sam crossed her arms and glowered at the rows of garishly colored boxes of breakfast cereal. "He's a big grump."

"Takes one to know one." Lia put a box of corn flakes into the cart. "Besides, he hasn't invited us and I doubt that he will." She worried her lip, reading over the list she'd made of the items that Jake had reeled off while he'd handed her a wad of twenties, more than enough for groceries. The thick lump of cash in her pocket only reminded her how much she'd come to count on Rose's hospitality as her meager savings had dwindled on the trip north.

"Then where will we go?"

Lia sighed. "I don't know."

"Do you have any money left?"

While Lia had tried as best she could to shield the children from their circumstances, Sam was aware. In the past year, she'd heard "I don't have the money for that" so often from Lia that she no longer asked for luxuries. She'd taken babysitting jobs and saved for months to buy the iPod.

"What if he does? Will you say yes?"

"Sam, please. I don't know."

"Well, you'd better decide," Sam said snottily.

Lia meant to scold her daughter's tone, but when their eyes met, she read Sam's distress despite her daughter's attempt to keep up the tough front. Another piece of Lia's heart chipped away.

"We'll be okay," she soothed. "Rose said rent is cheap in Alouette. If I can find a job, we'll manage."

"I can get a job and give you the money."

"I appreciate the offer, but you're only fourteen."

"So? I can work." Sam unzipped her backpack. "I have thirty-six dollars saved from babysitting. You can have it—to pay for a motel."

Lia wanted to refuse. She'd promised herself that she'd make it on her own from here on out.

Get real. The only way you'll make it is with Rose's help—now Jake's—and maybe Sam's babysitting money, too. Her pride hurt, but she'd been humbled before and she could do it again to give the kids the basics of food, shelter, safety. And eventually, she hoped, a better life.

"Thanks, honey," Lia said. "I may need a loan, but you hold on to your money for now."

Sam clutched the backpack. "I don't want to stay in those stinky cabins." Her voice was shrill.

"We'll see." Fighting to stay on an even keel despite her daughter's pushing, Lia rolled the cart into the next aisle. She met up with Howie and Kristen, who'd gone to get milk and eggs.

Howie put the cartons in the wire buggy. "I got two percent—is that okay, Mom?"

Kristen had glimpsed the cereal boxes around the corner. "Mommy, Mommy, Mom." She grabbed at Lia's shirt, untucking it again. "Can we have Honey-bear Crunch? Pleeese?"

Something a little like hysteria crawled up Lia's

throat. *At four ninety-five a box?* she wanted to screech. She pried her hand off the cart handle and took her daughter's shoulder to aim her at the toothpaste-and-soap aisle. Nothing there she'd want. "No cereal. We're not shopping for ourselves this time."

"Mr. Bubble!" Kristen took off like a shot.

"Howie?"

"I'll get her, Mom." He trudged after his sister.

Sam was staring at the floor. "Can we go now?"

Lia consulted the list. "Just a few more things."

"Mo-om. Come on, already." Sam stamped a clog. "I hate this stupid town. Why did you bring us here?" When Lia didn't answer, she flung herself into the next aisle.

"Get paper plates," Lia said matter-of-factly.

A roundly pregnant woman with a heaped cart gave Lia a wry look as she wheeled by. "Ah, the joys of motherhood. I can't wait."

"Your first?"

"Yes." The woman rubbed her belly, her face serene. "Due in a few more months."

Lia felt a pang. She remembered touching her ex's hand over her belly that way, with Samantha, when they were young and still in love. "Good luck," she said, moving on.

The woman looked past her shoulder. She was tall and queenly, with a burnished brunette bob and a wide smile. "You're new in town."

Lia paused. "Is it that obvious?"

"Only in Alouette. I've lived here for just about a

year now and already I'm on a first-name basis with
the entire population." She added chummily, "And you
have to wave at them every time your cars pass or
they'll think you're mad."

"Then you'd know—" Lia broke off. She had to
remember not to be forthcoming.

The woman looked curious, but she covered the
awkward silence by introducing herself. "I'm Claire
Saari."

"Lia Howard. We're not…uh, I'm not sure, but—"
She took control of her stumbling tongue. "What I'm
trying to say is that we may be only visiting overnight.
I haven't decided."

"Where are you staying?" When Lia hesitated to
answer, Claire laughed. "Sorry. I could blame small-
town nosiness, but really it's that there aren't many ac-
commodations in town and I run one of them." She
produced a card from her purse. "Bay House, a bed-
and-breakfast. June is early in the season yet, so I can
get you a room if you're looking."

Lia studied the card, which was embossed with a
line drawing of a Victorian mansion perched on a cliff-
side. Too ritzy by far. "Must be a nice place."

Claire lowered her voice. "I'll give you a discount."

"Thanks. I'll, uh, keep that in mind."

Claire glanced at the food in Lia's cart. "Your only
other local choice may not be viable, but you might
prefer it if they're open. Maxine's Cottages." She
pointed. "Thataway—on Blackbear Road."

"I know it."

"Oh. You've been there already? With most of the family away, I wasn't sure if the cottages—" Claire stopped and looked at Lia with dawning knowledge. "Wait a minute. You're Rose's friend from below the bridge, aren't you? I remember she mentioned a Lia who couldn't be at the wedding and so she had Tess as her maid of honor instead."

"This really is a small town," Lia said with some dread. What had possessed her to believe that she would be able to keep her secrets here? Except that Rose had managed for a very long time—until the man she'd wound up marrying had persuaded her that she could come clean.

"Yes." Claire had laughing eyes. "We're terribly small and gossipy. But we don't hold a grudge if you tell us to butt out when we get too intrusive. Like me now." She started to wheel her cart away, then stopped again. "Call me if you need anything, all right?"

"I had car trouble," Lia blurted. It was good to have an honest excuse. "That's why we missed the wedding. And now we're here and Rose is gone."

Claire made a sympathetic tsking sound. "You have to stick around until she comes back. I'm sure she'd want to see you."

"I'd like to, but…"

"Rose's brother should be at the cottages. I heard he's planning to renovate them and reopen."

"We met him already, the kids and I."

"Of course." Claire nodded at the groceries in the basket. "Then you are staying? Rose will be so pleased. She's not one to gush, but I could tell she'd really hoped to have you at the wedding."

"We'd been out of touch for a while." Lia was dismayed that she'd been thinking mostly of herself and how Rose could help her out of a dire situation.

But that had been their pattern as friends, since Rose had always been so cussedly independent, even taciturn, about her own desires. Lia was still having a hard time wrapping her head around the idea of the gruff woman she'd known marrying the town's widowed basketball coach and making a family that included his daughter and the teenage son Rose had given up for adoption when she was young.

"A few years apart doesn't matter between friends," said Claire. She tipped her head. "What did you think of Jake?"

Lia gulped down the thickness that formed in her throat at every thought of him. "He's a lot like Rose."

"The old Rose." Claire's eyes narrowed slightly as she considered Lia. "Maybe the new Rose, too."

What did that mean? Lia didn't want to ask because she suspected the observation involved her and the kids. "I don't know the new Rose."

"She's much like the old one except she smiles more often and even carries on a conversation. She has a great rapport with Lucy, her new stepdaughter."

"Uh-huh. She was always good with my kids. I

have three." Lia lifted her head to the sound of the trio squabbling in the next aisle of the small grocery store. She gave a wry smile. "That's them. I'd better go."

"Tell Jake I said hi."

"Sure." Lia made a hurried wave and wheeled away, her face growing warm as she puzzled over the idea of how Jake might be like the newly married, newly mothered Rose. The likeliest explanation was too absurd to hold in her head. She shook it loose. Crazy. Although she barely knew the man, she was certain that Jake was not the family type.

Pretty certain.

CHAPTER THREE

TWENTY MINUTES LATER, Lia poured a sixty-four-ounce can of tomato juice over Jake's head. The thick red waterfall coated his hair and face, then streamed in slimy globules over his shoulders and chest. He was stoic, not making a sound as she shook the can and the last droplets landed all over his face.

"Cool," Howie said. "It looks like blood. Dump some on me."

"Ugh." Lia cranked open another can.

Jake used a washcloth to smear the juice over his skin. He and Howie sat in a big iron claw-foot tub. Howie had insisted on the communal bath, which was unusual because he'd always been a serious little guy, private about his personal business from an early age. Lia had expected Jake to refuse or at least hesitate, but he'd merely shrugged and climbed into the tub in his boxers. It was the same with the grocery receipt and remaining cash that she'd carefully laid out on the kitchen table so he could see she'd accounted for every penny. He'd barely spared a glance. Jake certainly wasn't a fussy man.

Not like Larry.

"Sauce me," Howie said.

"*Seinfeld,*" Jake said. "The entity."

Howie pumped a fist, making a splash in the pink water. "Yes!"

"What did I miss?" Lia dumped juice over Howie's head. He shrieked and sputtered with delight. She smiled to hear it, and her lungs expanded, taking in a deeper breath than she'd known for months, even years.

Jake leaned back in the tub. "Don't you ever watch *Seinfeld* reruns?"

"Not really."

"See, there was this episode with a stink in the car, called 'the entity,'" Howie said, forgetting to breathe he was so excited.

"The stink clung to everything it touched," Jake added.

"So Elaine, her hair smelled, and she had to get a tomato-juice shampoo, and she said—"

"Sauce me," Jake and Howie chorused. They looked at Lia, waiting for a laugh.

"I see." She shook the empty can. "But this is juice, not sauce."

"Mom."

"Same thing." Jake shook his head at Howie. "She doesn't get it."

Howie shook his head at Lia. "You don't get it, Mom."

"I guess not." She caught Jake's eye and lifted an eyebrow. "Seeing as you're the man with so much stinkin' entity experience, how fast does this remedy work?"

Jake sniffed himself. "We stay in as long as it takes."

Howie leaned forward to get a whiff. "I smell tomato juice."

Lia took a pitcher of water and poured it over her son's sandy-colored head. "You're going to have pink hair."

Howie wasn't sure how to take that news. "Jake, too?"

"His hair is dark. The tomato won't stain as much."

Jake passed her a bottle of shampoo. Lia snapped it open and squeezed out a dollop. She began massaging the lather into Howie's hair and scalp, but he pushed her away. "I can do it."

"Want to wash mine?" Jake's question seemed serious—until Lia detected the smile in the laugh lines carved around his eyes. He had a very masculine face—strong bones, blunt features, a firm jaw bristling with a five-o'clock shadow. His dark hair was peppered with gray.

"I'm sure you're capable." She collected the cans and can opener. "I'll leave you two to finish up. Howie, rinse off thoroughly. I don't want to find sticky tomato juice behind your ears."

Jake saluted. "We'll proceed accordingly and present ourselves for inspection, ma'am. Right, Howie?"

"Yes, sir." Howie saluted with a sudsy hand.

Lia smiled at them. "Here are your glasses, Howie."

She placed the spectacles on the surround of a chipped white sink of fifties vintage and caught sight of herself in the mirrored medicine cabinet. Her hair was as fuzzy as a played-out Barbie doll's. The touch of lipstick and mascara she'd applied that morning was long gone. She looked bone-tired and at least ten years older than thirty-two.

She turned her face aside. Some days she felt that old. But not right now. Being around Jake was rejuvenating. He put out a lot of rugged male energy. Her spirits perked up and her body responded whether or not she wanted it to. Even though she was usually not focused on that stuff, him being half-naked most of the time was mighty distracting.

The girls were hovering outside the door to the bathroom. "When can we leave?" Sam asked.

Kristen tugged on Lia's hand and said plaintively, "I'm hungry."

Lia mouthed, "Quiet," and hustled both of them toward the kitchen. The stone house was small—two bedrooms, one bath, with a fairly roomy kitchen that opened onto an L-shaped dining and living room area. Though neat as a pin, the kitchen showed the wear and tear of time on the scuffed linoleum, ancient fixtures and stained ceramic sink. A pair of faded print curtains hung in the window that overlooked the new garden and the stand of evergreens that crested the riverbank. Altogether, it was a homely but homey place. Lia wished she could curl into a fetal position on the sagging plaid couch and sleep for the next twenty-four hours.

The shower was running. Jake shouldn't have been able to overhear, but Lia spoke quickly in a low voice nevertheless. "Samantha, we will go as soon as we can." *Even though I don't know where we're going.* "Krissy, baby…" She sank onto her heels and gave her youngest a quick hug. "Dinner's coming. Eat a few animal crackers to tide you over."

The box of cookies hung from a string wound around Kristen's finger. Her stuffed rabbit, Cuddle-bunny, was clutched in the other hand. "They're gone." She was on the verge of tears, a sure sign that she was overtired. "Sam ate 'em all."

"I did not."

"Did, too! I said she could have one of the elephants and she taked a big handful."

"Girls, shhh. It's okay." Lia pinched between her eyes. "I won't let you starve." She looked at Jake's cash on the table and thought of the food he'd placed just so in the almost bare cupboards. At the store, she'd counted out her remaining coins to pay for the animal crackers. There was still her credit card, but they could be tracked through that. She didn't want to use it unless she had no other choice.

One look at Kristen's welling eyes said that point may have been reached. Lia's head drooped. She put a hand on the floor to steady herself. Running away from home in the Grudge with less than four hundred dollars in cash had been a foolish decision but necessary. Absolutely necessary.

Except where did they go now?

"Help yourselves," Jake said from the hallway.

Lia pulled herself together and stood on shaky legs. Weak from hunger, she told herself. Not just weak.

To Jake, she said, "I'm sorry. You know children. Or maybe you don't. They get weepy when they're hungry and I—" She let out a choked-off laugh. She was feeling kind of weepy and hopeless herself.

Even though he spoke easily, Jake's grip tightened on the towel he'd draped around his shoulders. "No problem. I'll get dressed and we'll make dinner."

Lia opened her mouth but didn't speak. She was in no position to refuse. "You're being very kind, considering how we barged in on you." Their eyes met and she cringed inside, reading his expression as pity. She didn't want pity. She wanted respect. Independence.

But first, dinner. "Thank you."

After a nudge, Kristen and Sam chimed in. "Thank you, Mr. Robbin."

He brushed off the gratitude in his abrupt way. So much like Rose. "All of you—call me Jake," he said before disappearing into one of the bedrooms.

"I NOTICE YOUR MOTHER isn't here," Lia commented in the careful tones of a guest bent on making polite conversation. "I know Rose has been caring for her for the past few years."

Jake rolled a beer bottle between his palms. He was sprawled in one of the Adirondack chairs they kept around for the cottage guests—when they had any. The grill smoked nearby as the charcoal cooled. He'd given Lia a choice of hamburgers or fresh-caught fish. She'd chosen the fish, to her offspring's displeasure. They'd been polite about eating at least some of it and had filled up on corn on the cob and the biscuits Lia had produced after scouting his kitchen for flour and baking powder.

Jake met her inquiring eyes. "Maxine…uh, my mother is in the hospital."

"I'm sorry to hear that. Nothing too serious, I hope."

"She got overwrought and her emphysema worsened."

"Too much wedding excitement?"

"In a way. More a case of the wedding demanding too much of my sister's attention. If you knew our mother, you'd understand." While no one in their household had ruled the roost but Black Jack, his mother had become passive-aggressive to get her way. Particularly with Rose.

Jake glanced at Lia. "Or do you know? I forget that Rose might've confided in you about the history of our family."

"She told me some of it. But not everything. Not even close."

"That sounds like Rose."

After a minute of silence, Lia cleared her throat. "Will your mother be home soon?"

"Not right away. She's being moved to a care facility. They want to monitor her for a while longer. Of course, she's putting up a fuss, but making her stay was the only way for the newlyweds to get a honeymoon. If she was here, she'd have insisted that Rose stick around to look after her." Jake was bemused by his loose tongue. After the goings-on of the wedding, he'd been looking forward to solitude. But having Lia and her kids around wasn't so bad. "I was never much good at that sort of thing—caretaking. No patience."

"You were great with Howie."

"I've worked at staying calm under pressure."

"In the Army, huh." She did a marching-in-place gesture that made him smile. "All that discipline."

He nodded.

"Well," Lia said after a minute, searching for another topic when he would have been fine to sit with her in silence, "family illness hasn't been an issue for me. My parents are young yet, in their midfifties." She looked down and picked at a fingernail. "We're not close."

"How come?" he asked after a beat. Talking like this made him slightly uncomfortable. He didn't believe in revealing your feelings to passing strangers—or even lingering strangers. Hell, he didn't even talk to his own brother. He'd tried to stay in touch with Gary after the prison sentence, but there was too much anger and resentment there. Jake and Lia had found ways to straighten themselves out. Gary was a casualty.

"They didn't approve of me marrying so young." Lia laughed a little to cover the obvious pain. "Not that they would have approved of me having a baby out of wedlock, either."

"I thought that in these cases, once the grandchild arrives, the grandparents come around."

"You'd think so." She sighed. "I mean, yes, they have made an effort with their grandkids. We visit back and forth a few times a year. But they never quite let me forget what a disappointment I've been, including the divorce."

There was another, longer silence. "Rose—a newly-wed," Lia said suddenly with a fond smile. He could tell she was deliberately lightening the mood. "Incredible."

"Evan seems like a good guy."

"He'd better be."

Jake liked Lia's fierce loyalty. He'd felt that way about his battalion. Good guys, most of them, and excellent soldiers. With his mother and sister, the family ties were tangled up in turmoil and guilt. He hadn't been able to protect them the way he'd have liked to. But then, that way would have likely resulted in his own prison sentence. Back when they'd needed him the most, the only solutions he'd known involved hot temper and flying fists.

Black Jack's legacy. Like father, like son.

Jake slapped a mosquito that had landed on his arm. He wiped away the bloody smear and lifted the beer, tipping it toward Lia. "You're sure you don't want one?"

"Not tonight. I'm too tired. A beer would put me right to sleep." She looked at the sun slipping past the tops of the looming evergreens. "We should be going before it gets dark," she said, but didn't move.

"Where to?"

"Um…" Her lids lowered. "I met a woman at the grocery store. Claire. She gave me her card, said we could get a room at her bed-and-breakfast."

"Free?"

"Well, no, I don't suppose so." Lia's face crumpled. She looked miserable whenever the question of money came up. He assumed she had very little, maybe none given that she'd balked over the price of tomato juice, but apparently pride wouldn't let her admit it.

He could understand that. Pride—and hurt pride— had caused him a lot of grief back in the day.

"You might as well stay here," he said. His voice came out raspy and gruff, making the offer less than inviting even though he didn't mean it that way.

Lia gazed across the property, taking in the small cottages hidden among the trees. Birds twittered in the gap before she spoke again. "I don't want to disrupt your business."

He snorted. "What business?"

"There are no guests?"

"We've got a few diehards scheduled for later in the season. I'm planning to have the place fixed up some by then." He tried to soften his voice. "I can give you one of the cottages for as long as you need it. No problem."

Lia closed her eyes and pressed her lips together, taking a breath through her nose. "We'd—I'd be so grateful."

"I don't need gratitude for doing what Rose would want." Jake figured he owed his sister, not Lia. He drained the bottle and set it on the ground beside his chair, then resettled himself, stretching out full length with his arms folded behind his head. "Your car shouldn't be on the road anyway. I took a look under the hood while you were at the store. You've got bad brakes. The struts need replacing. Front tires are bald, too."

Lia's face got that pale, drained look again. "That sounds expensive. I'm not sure the Grudge is worth that much repair. But I need a car." She glanced his way. "Are you a mechanic?"

"Not as a profession. But I can do the work."

"I couldn't ask you to."

"You didn't." He eyed her. How could one small woman be so uptight and wrung-out at the same time? He'd seen from the start that there was something off about her arrival. Through dinner, she'd hushed the kids whenever they'd mentioned their previous life, which had only called his attention to her evasiveness.

Jake wasn't one to wait for explanations. But he sensed that Lia would bolt if he got too curious. This once, he could bide his time.

"What I meant was that I can't pay you," she said.

"I didn't ask to be paid. We can figure something out. Do you have a job to get back to?"

"No." She was studying her lap again. "I quit my job. I was actually hoping to find work up here."

"In Alouette?" That explained the car stuffed with luggage and boxes. He'd figured them for heavy travelers.

"Maybe." She shot him an arch glance. "Don't worry. We won't count on your generosity forever. Just until I get a paycheck and can find a place to rent."

"It's not so easy getting a job in this town. What do you do?"

"I'll do anything." She moved restlessly. "I don't have specialized training or a degree. I managed only a few college courses after Sam was born, before Lar—" She cut herself off again. "Since the divorce, I've worked at several jobs. Supermarket checker, office clerk for a used-car dealer, waitress. I'll find something."

"Sure."

"You sound skeptical."

"It's a small town. I can ask around for you, but I've been out of touch for too long. Been back only a few weeks."

"Thanks, but that's not necessary," she said. "I'll go out tomorrow, first thing. There has to be some kind of job available for an untrained single mom." She smiled bravely. Tension radiated off her.

He leaned forward. "No rush."

"Maybe not to you, but I'm in a fix."

"You said you're divorced?"

"Yeah. For about three years now officially, but we were separated before that. I was pregnant with Kristen when we moved out of our house and next door to Rose. She was a good friend to me while I had the baby and went through the divorce mess. My ex fought it, so, uh, the process took a while."

He sensed a world of complication in the brief explanation. He had some vague memory of getting the rare letter from his sister that mentioned Lia, but he hadn't paid close attention to the details. Now he wished he had. Something about her engaged his interest more than other women. Maybe the fortitude he sensed beneath her exhaustion. If he ever got involved again, it would be with a woman who had staying power.

He continued to probe despite his usual disinterest in chitchat. "Don't the wife and kids usually get the house?"

Lia winced. "Not always."

"He was a son of a bitch, huh?"

"To put it mildly." Lia glanced over her shoulder. "We're well rid of him."

Jake's radar went *ping*. The look in her eyes…was it hunted, not haunted?

Stay out of it, man. "I'm sure you'll be okay from now on," he said, feeling as if he was mouthing a useless platitude.

She clutched her arms tight and shook her head.

"Yes, you will." He'd see to it.

Jake bit back a groan. His resistance was low for damsels in distress. Always had been, even at age nine, when he'd attacked his own dad for yelling at his mother. He'd earned a cuffing for that, one that had taken out a couple of loose baby teeth.

"Right," Lia said, worn out but taking hold. "Of course. We'll be fine." She cocked her head, listening to the sound of the TV inside the house, where her two youngest were ensconced on the couch. Behind them, Sam was hunkered down in the car, attached to her iPod, reclining in the backseat with her feet dangling out the window.

"We'll be fine," Lia repeated, trying to convince herself.

Jake got to his feet before he found himself offering not only a house but his left arm, too, if it'd take the trouble from her eyes. "We should check out the cottage. It might need freshening up." Plus a bug bomb, mousetraps and a scrub brush.

He sniffed his hand, then held it out to Lia to help her up from the low-slung chair. She complied readily, though her small laugh sounded uncomfortable and she let go as soon as she was on her feet.

"Do I still smell of skunk?" he asked. He'd been cutting onions and squeezing lemons for the fish.

She grinned. "You smell like an especially pungent spaghetti sauce."

"Great." He pointed to the first cottage to the west of the main house. "Here's the one you want. It's the biggest." As they walked by the car, Sam's blue-tipped head popped up. She'd probably snap if he told her she looked like a blue jay.

Her glare bored holes into Jake's skull, but he'd been glowered at by a two-star general with a Napoleon complex and hadn't backed down. One sullen teenager could be conquered. Not that he had any intentions of getting involved in their lives beyond today.

"Thank you for being so sweet to Howie," Lia said on the crumbling cement doorstep. "And the rest of us." She held the creaky screen door while he put his shoulder to the wooden door that had swollen shut.

It flew open and Jake's boot thudded onto the dusty floorboards. He coughed. "Sweet? What's that? Hell, woman, I've got a reputation to maintain."

Lia wasn't having any. "In case you didn't notice, my son's kinda dazzled by you. You're like a G.I. Joe doll brought to life." She continued past Jake's snort of disapproval. "Anyway, I appreciate your tolerance. I'll try to keep him out of your way as much as possible while we're here."

"He's no trouble."

She laughed drily. "You say that now, but just wait."

Jake brandished a hand at the interior of the house. "What do you think? It's not much, but at least there's a working bathroom and two double beds."

The cottage had a couple of rooms, plus the small

bath. They'd stepped into the living room area, furnished by a thrift-store sofa and two of the rustic twig armchairs his father used to build in the off-season. Uncomfortable as hell for sitting. A couple of cabinets, a tiny sink, mini fridge and microwave made do as the kitchen. Thick stone walls and small paned windows overhung with ivy and climbing roses made the room seem dark and unappealing to Jake. He switched on the lone hanging light—a cast-iron chandelier with yellowed lampshades festooned with cobwebs.

Lia saw differently. "Oh, wow. It's charming, Jake. A real storybook cottage."

He drew a line through the dust on the floor. "Needs a good cleaning."

"I can do that. In fact..." She poked her head inside the bedroom, where two iron bedsteads were pushed up against the walls, sparing only enough room for an old pine dresser and a night table with a birch-bark lamp. She withdrew. Her bright eyes fixed on Jake. "I can clean all the cottages for you. In return for rent, as long as we stay. Maybe even afterward, if you need me as part-time help. How does that sound?"

He bobbed his head. "Like a deal."

Immediately he could see that the discouragement weighing her down had lightened considerably. She bounded forward and shook his hand. "Deal."

He didn't let go as easily as he had earlier. Maybe three seconds, that's all it was, but color leaped into her cheeks and she made a breath-catching sound as she pulled away.

Jake resisted the urge to clench his fingers. He knew chemistry when he felt it. Taking on three kids and a single mom was bad enough, but that complication he did not need, unless it led only to a fast, uncomplicated lay. He was betting that a cheap lay was strictly off-limits with Lia. Especially with her kids around.

So back off now, man. You don't need this.

Of course, that wasn't what Rose had been saying since Jake's return, with all her teasing about him following suit and finding a good woman and settling down. He'd claimed that her brain had turned into romantic mush because of the wedding, but maybe she had a point.

He was thirty-nine and regimented in his ways. If he was ever going to give the marriage-and-family thing a legitimate shot, it should be soon. Never in his wildest dreams had he imagined hooking up with a woman with three kids, especially when everything about them spelled trouble. Yet there was a certain efficiency about the situation that suddenly appealed, regardless of his ingrained habit of detachment.

Maybe he was thinking crazy, but suddenly he saw that with Lia he might be able to skip all that romance and courting malarkey in favor of forming a mutually beneficial alliance. One tight family unit, based on function rather than emotion. Emotion wasn't reliable. Neither was sexual attraction. He'd learned that the hard way.

Most women wouldn't go for a practical union,

even if they were in dire straits. But Lia had already learned marriage wasn't pretty, and divorce even uglier. She might be ready to listen to reason.

Jake recognized that he was jumping the gun. Still, the notion wouldn't let go.

One stop, no shopping.

A ready-made family.

CHAPTER FOUR

BY ALL RIGHTS, LIA should have slept like the prover-
bial log, six of which Jake had hauled into the cottage
and set up in the woodstove in the corner, saying they
could have a fire if they got chilly at night. He'd
showed her how to arrange the kindling and the logs
and open the damper, with a fascinated Howie
hovering nearby, taking everything in.

But it wasn't the cool northern air that kept Lia
from sleep or even the nightmare she sometimes had
about being followed and cornered by a menacing
figure. She'd have almost preferred the nightmare. No
question where it came from.

Nope, what had awakened her from an already less-
than-sound sleep was the disturbing way Jake had
looked at her after they'd struck the deal about the
cottage. Sober, speculative, far too intense. As if he'd
seen something about her, something surprising, something…secret.

Had he guessed about Larry?

Icy prickles slid along her spine at the possibility
and what that could mean if Jake was a law-and-order

type. She hadn't figured him out on that point. His military experience said he'd operate by the book and turn her in. Yet there was also an untamed, renegade aura about him. Vestiges of the wild brother from Rose's tales of their adolescence, she assumed. Prone to fisticuffs and breaking the law.

Quietly Lia slid from the bed and into her robe.

The other possibility of what Jake had been thinking flickered at the back of her brain like a moth at the screen door. She couldn't seem to brush it away.

It's nothing. Just a biological urge. You've been without a man for too long.

She and Rose used to call themselves reluctant nuns. They'd goad each other into accepting occasional dates and then pick apart the poor men afterward, calling them "the slobberer," "the mama's boy," "the braggart," discarding them as if the two women were such prize catches themselves.

But Jake...

He was a man. A real man. A man's man. The kind of guy she'd always been intimidated by, which was how she'd wound up with Larry, the supposed nice boy.

Stop it. You're making too much of nothing. It was just one look.

She glanced at Kristen and Samantha. Sleeping like angels. Even Sam had been too tired—or too resigned—to complain about sharing a bed. Lia pulled the blankets up to Howie's chin. He looked naked without his glasses. Younger, too. At times she forgot that he was only ten. Having a good, strong male influence like Jake in his life, if only for a short while, would be invaluable to him.

Jake. He simply refused to leave her mind.

She belted the robe and quietly let herself out of the cottage, easing the screen door shut on her fingertips. The trees grew together so thickly they cast one big, deep shadow, but dawn glowed between the uppermost branches.

Lia shivered on the doorstep in her stocking feet. So what if Jake had looked at her? He hadn't said a word. Yet she couldn't deny that she'd been shaken. She'd covered up by making a production about rounding up the kids, sweeping out the cottage, bringing in their gear.

She closed her eyes, sucked in the fresh, fragrant air. *You're on your own. Truly on your own. You can make it.*

"I heard the screen door. Couldn't sleep?"

Lia's lids flew open. Jake stood on the path, wearing a thermal shirt with the sleeves pushed up, his hands tucked in the pockets of a pair of jeans. God, he looked good.

"I'm antsy, I guess."

"Want some coffee? I've got a pot brewing."

"Love some." She stepped down. "You're an early riser."

"Habit."

She sucked in a breath. "Smells good."

His mouth twisted. "Me?"

Her eyes widened. "The coffee."

"I took another bath."

"I'm sure you smell good, too, but forget it—I'm not sniffing you again."

He chuckled. "Follow me."

She scurried after him, the pine needles sticking to her socks. Only fifteen or twenty feet separated the houses.

He saw her glance back. "The kids'll be fine. Nothing dangerous here."

"Except skunks." An eerie call came from the trees. Lia shivered and moved closer to Jake. "What was that?"

"Owl."

"It's a lonesome sound."

"Usually there's a response from across the river." They waited in silence. Nothing but the chipping sounds of tiny birds that hopped from branch to branch.

"Not this time," he said, holding the door open for her.

She darted inside, feeling unsettled again. *I'll draw the lines,* she told herself. No matter how much of an outlaw Jake had been as a young man, he was now the type who'd respect boundaries. She'd be clear that her purpose was to find a job and a home. Not a man.

Jake poured her a mug and put it on the kitchen table. She sat. He took out the milk carton, a sugar bowl. She poked at the solid lump of sugar, scraping off a spoonful.

"I want to make it on my own," she blurted.

He was leaning against the edge of the counter, the flat of one hand tucked inside his belt. He looked at her and blinked. "Sure."

"I know. I'm not on my own. Not yet."

He shrugged. "I told you. Take your ti—"

"I don't want to take my time." She sounded as petulant as Sam, but she went on. "I want to prove I can do this. I have to."

Jake mulled while she sipped the hot coffee, grateful for the sting on her tongue, the shot of caffeine to her bloodstream.

"I thought you've been on your own for four years."

"Yes, but—" She pressed her tongue to her teeth. How could she explain about Larry and his constant intrusiveness without raising too many red flags? She didn't want to be saved by Jake in that way, either, attractive as the prospect might be at times.

"It's been a struggle," she said. "And I've had to take money from my ex-husband."

"Child support, alimony—you're owed that."

"Legally, yes. It's more complicated in reality. When Larry doles out money, it comes with strings." She wound her feet around the chair rungs, not looking at Jake. Let him think that she'd gone through your garden-variety messy divorce, not one that had led to threats, stalking, restraining orders and potentially an arrest.

"So you came up here to get away from him?"

"More or less."

Jake tilted his mug, watching her from beneath a furrowed brow. "Won't he want to see the kids?"

"He doesn't really care," she said a bit breathlessly. She was lying, although it wasn't the kids that he cared about as much as what they represented. Custody and visitation had been Larry's trump card. He'd manipulated Lia through his demands about the children from day one of the separation, using them at every opportunity, wrangling for more time, frequent holidays, then ignoring them or cruelly twisting their minds with his bitter lies and schemes.

Lia kept all that off her face as she looked up at Jake. "What I'm trying to say is that I've had it with men. I'm not looking for a relationship. I want to be left alone to find my own way."

He put down his coffee. "Sounds good."

"Oh."

"You'll get no argument from me."

"Okay."

"I've always preferred an uncomplicated life."

"Then we—we're—" She waved her hands. The heat from the coffee had gone into her face.

"On the same page," Jake said, his voice relaxed, his expression untroubled.

Cripes. Had she read him totally wrong? Every feminine instinct she possessed shouted no.

"Great," she said, uncertain whether her instincts

were operating correctly after so many years of Larry. He'd been her first and only boyfriend. None of the men from the reluctant nun dates had lasted long enough to be called relationships.

She took a nervous gulp from the mug. The discussion with Jake had gone too smoothly. She wasn't used to a straightforward meeting of the minds. She didn't trust it. With Larry, compliance only meant that he was plotting in a different direction, planning to slither onto another path. She saw Jake more as a bull moose who'd crash down her door with one big bam if he'd set his mind on having her. But still...

She stood. "I have to shower and change. Job search."

"Luck," he grunted. Mr. Laconic.

She gave him a wave.

He stopped her at the front door. "Take my truck."

"No, thanks. The Grudge will have to do for tooling around town." Another problem occurred to her, however, then another. Fantastic. All her talk about being independent and she needed nothing but favors from him.

She made herself speak. "I do need your help with something else."

"At your service."

"Can I use your home phone number as my contact? I don't have a cell phone." Sam found the lack an utter embarrassment to her existence as a twenty-first-century teenager.

"Go ahead." Jake reeled off the numbers.

"And…" Lia clenched her lapels. "Is it okay if I leave the kids here while I'm in town? Samantha will be in charge, and I'll instruct them not to wander off, but if you could check in occasionally that would ease my mind. You know, see that they haven't gone swimming or encountered another skunk or set fire to Kristen's hair. That is, if you were going to be around anyway. I should be back in a few hours."

Though Jake looked dubious, he said, "I'll be here. You might want to tell Sam that she's second in command."

"Uh, okay." Lia frowned. He liked to have control. At least he was up front about it, where Larry had been insidious. She had to repress a shudder anyway.

"Wait a minute." Jake disappeared, then came back with the sugar bowl, box of corn flakes and carton of milk. Even a plastic bottle of orange juice. He dumped the items on Lia. "For their breakfast."

Her resistance melted into gratefulness. What was she thinking? Regardless of the gruff exterior, he was obviously a very thoughtful man.

"Thanks." She stepped outside, then stopped. The eastern sky had turned to lemon, pink and lavender, like rainbow sherbet. "So you're probably thinking that all my talk about making it on my own was baloney, but, really, it wasn't. I meant it." She cast him a quick glance and was met with the stone face again. "And the other thing, too. No rom—no relationships."

"Fine by me."

Ah, they were back to monosyllables. She said, "Me, too," and then an awkward, "'Bye," before hurrying away along the path.

Jake leaned a shoulder against the doorjamb, watching her with an aggravatingly bemused expression on his smug mug.

Lia recognized that she was out of sorts with no good reason. Except that, considering the look he'd given her yesterday, Jake was being altogether too agreeable.

He'd stirred her like a cup of coffee. Even with a spoonful of sugar, swallowing the dose of medicine she'd doled out to herself wasn't easy.

"I HATE IT HERE," SAM said to the treetops. Howie and Kristen were watching TV in Jake's house, their eyes glazed over like androids plugged into an electromatron. She'd escaped to the forest, which was horrible, all scratchy and twiggy and buggy, but at least she was alone.

"I hate my mom," she said, then felt guilty and added, "for bringing me here."

Sam stomped her feet, pretending that she was squashing bugs when really she just had to get her frustration out. Finally she dropped to her knees in the long grass and started tearing up big handfuls, flinging them in every direction. She'd have busted out into tears if she was the emo type, but she wasn't. She was cool. All her friends said that.

Sam Pogue was ice.

She dashed at a tear threatening to escape.

Even the glaciers were melting. Stupid global warming.

"I wa-a-ant to go home," she said, putting a wah-wah in it, letting herself wallow in misery since no one was watching.

But did she? Home wasn't such a great place to be either, especially with her dad pulling his stunts and her mom always nervous or having to go to family court. Sam wanted her friends and she wanted her room even though she had to share it with Kristen. They lived in a crappy two-bedroom apartment in the worst part of town, but Sam had made that work for her once she'd realized that she'd never be a boppy little cheerleader or fashion-obsessed princess.

So she'd become a gal from the 'hood. A tough chick. A little bit Goth. She dressed in black and she was getting a tattoo as soon as she turned eighteen. Probably a whole bunch of them. Maybe even before she was eighteen. She'd already talked her dad into letting her get the piercing below her lip.

Mom had freaked. She'd made Sam take out the stud, only Sam had put it back every time her mom was out of sight until finally she'd worn her mom down.

But no tattoos. Not yet.

If only her mom had taken them somewhere cool, like Mexico. Or Argentina. They could have been real outlaws. Except it was hard to stay on the run when you had Kristen whining for chocolate milk and her stuffed animals, and Howie calculating mileage so they didn't run out of gas in the middle of nowhere.

Sam flung herself flat on the ground. There was so much sky here. It was too big, blue and clear to be believed. But that was only because this was Nowhere-ville. The absolute end of the world.

Her mom was so lame. She didn't even know how to run away. Even if this was a nothing little town where nothing ever happened, they could still be found so easy. If her mom had bothered to ask Sam, she could have told how to give them all new identities. She'd looked it up online.

They probably didn't even have text messaging in this backward town. Probably they still listened to the Black-Eyed Peas and wore Vote for Pedro T-shirts. The kids would look at Sam like *she* was the freak because they didn't know any better.

So maybe she wouldn't go to school if they stayed here. She might run away instead. What could her mom do about it? She couldn't go to the police. She'd practically spazzed out when that dumb cop had walked up to the car to tell them their taillight was out.

Sam could pass for eighteen if she was on her own. She was sure of that. Almost sure. And she wouldn't fall for any of the usual runaway crap like drugs and prostitution. She was way too smart.

The sun felt good on her face and bare stomach. She

spread her arms and legs across the ground like a little kid making snow angels. If she ran away, she'd be free. No mom making rules, no dad making trouble, no brother and sister making her mad.

Except that she'd need a place to stay and a job. And if she didn't go to college, she'd end up like her mom, forever stuck in a drudge job with a junker car and thrift-shop clothes. Yuck.

Sam sprang up. Suddenly she had to run.

She tore through the woods and down the hill to the river, staying well out of sight of Jake, who'd said he'd be nearby at one of the stone houses, clearing brush. She could hear him hacking at something. Every once in a while an engine whined as he cut through the overgrowth.

His tattoos were kinda cool. But he was a big old grouch who thought he could boss Sam around. Every time he'd stuck his nose into the house to check on them like a prison guard, Sam had stared laser beams at him until he'd gone away.

Sam slowed. Her mom had said not to go near the river under any circumstances.

Too bad, so sad, I'm mad.

She picked her way along the riverbank, climbing in and out of thickets of long grass and cattails. Mosquitoes buzzed her head, and she slapped at them wildly, missing by a mile.

She stopped and leaned into the light breeze coming off the water. If she had a boat, she could sail away, at least for a while. Jake probably had one around somewhere.

The river curved just ahead. She climbed across a big rock, landing on a pebbled stretch of flat beach. Relieved to be walking normally, she trudged ahead with her hands stuffed in her jeans pockets.

At the sound of a splash, she looked up. Two teenage boys were fishing in the river. The tall, stocky one was wading onto shore. The other stood in the rushing water up to his hips with the line of his fishing pole drifting in the current. He was cute in a *Smallsville* kind of way, with dark curly hair and a tight bod. Kind of short for Sam, because she was tall for her age, but she didn't care about that when he looked up and smiled at her. He had a real nice smile.

Sam was itchy and sweaty. She wanted to turn and run. Instead she cocked one hip, ran her tongue against the back of the stud in her lip to remind herself how radical she was even if she was only fourteen and said with an ultracasual cool, "Hey."

LIA WANTED AN ICE cream cone. At that instant, she wanted one even more than she wanted never to hear another person say they had no openings, sorry, if only she'd applied earlier in the season. There were a few dollars from Sam in her purse. She'd borrowed them because applying for jobs without a dime to your name seemed wrong, for some odd reason, when it was actually quite appropriate.

Buying a cone would be frivolous and indulgent when her children were relying on the kindness of a tattooed Army Ranger for their lunch. Still, she couldn't talk herself out of the craving.

The day had turned sunny. The air was moist and sticky with humidity and the top of Lia's head was hot to the touch. Perspiration trickled from every pore. Even her tongue stuck to the roof of her mouth as she surveyed the Berry Dairy ice cream stand.

It was the typical small white-frame shack, tucked away in the corner of a parking lot between the wooded hillside and a square brick building that looked like a Monopoly hotel. Two white resin tables with striped umbrellas offered seating, but most of the customers were standing in a line that didn't seem to be moving.

Lia joined them, clutching her purse with both hands. She observed the crowd. Many were fresh off the beach, with damp swimsuits and sandy legs. The rest were dressed in shorts and tanks or T-shirts, except for one man in a shirt and tie dribbled with hot fudge.

She was out of place in her dark skirt and blouse and the sensible pumps that pinched her toes. Maybe after she got her cone she'd head down to the marina and sit on the seawall with her bare feet dangling in the water. She could ask the harbormaster if they needed someone to scrape gull guano off the moorings. As desperate as she felt, she'd probably snatch at even that job.

The line inched forward. Lia craned her neck. Only

one worker was scooping cones and making change—
a teenage girl who looked hot and cranky about being
stuck in a work space jammed with the big silver ice
cream machine and overstuffed shelves. A jumbo box
of cones had tipped over, spilling its contents on the
counter and floor. The window was sticky with hand-
prints. A wad of napkins had been stuffed halfway into
the dispenser. Every time a customer peeled one
off, several more fell to the cement. The napkins were
sticking to people's sandals and fluttering through
the parking lot.

Ten minutes later, Lia reached the window. "One
scoop of cherry on a plain cone."

"Sprinkles? Jimmies?" asked the harried worker.

"No, thanks." While she waited, Lia opened the dispenser and loaded the napkins correctly. She used one
to dab at blotches of melted ice cream on the window
ledge, but what she really needed was a sponge.

The girl handed Lia a cone. "Ninety-five cents."

Lia forked over a precious dollar. "I don't suppose
you've got a job opening."

"We sure do. My partner quit. She just up and quit
on me, no warning. Said she wanted to spend the
summer on the beach with her boyfriend. He's cheating
on her, but do I say anything, even though I'm left to
serve the noontime rush all on my own? Nope. I just
let her go."

Lia peered into the low opening. The girl had the
kind of full cheeks and button nose that would have

made for a cheerful face if she hadn't been so frazzled. She couldn't have been more than sixteen or seventeen. "You're doing the hiring?"

"Uh-huh. I'm the manager. Sarah Johnson. I've been here for three summers. Next, please."

Lia stepped aside while the customer was served. She licked her cone, taking another scan of the place. Was she really that desperate?

Every shop on the main street had said no. So had the grocery store, the township office, the post office and the diner down the street, which she'd thought had been her ace in the hole.

Sarah passed a double-scoop cone dipped in chocolate out the window.

Lia nudged back into view. "What's the pay?"

"Minimum wage. Thirty hours per week, give or take, including weekends. No benefits."

Lia slurped her ice cream before it dripped all over her hand. "I'd like to apply for the job."

"You?" Sarah blinked like a baby doll. "I thought you were asking for your daughter or son."

"I need a job."

"I don't know…"

"I want a triple-fudge shake," said a woman carrying a screaming toddler. "And Violet will have a cup of strawberry if the strawberries aren't too chunky. If they're too chunky, then make hers a strawberry shake, extra creamy."

Sarah took a step back, crushing cones underfoot.

Lia stuck her head into the opening. "I can start right away."

"You're hired."

CHAPTER FIVE

LIA'S LITTLE GIRL approached Jake with her thumb stuck in her mouth. She wasn't sucking it; she was nibbling on the nail. She took out the thumb to ask, "Where's my mommy?"

"She called. She's working. She'll be home soon."

When Kristen continued to stare up at him, he gave her a pat on the head. "Go find Sam."

"Sam said for me to go away."

Jake grumbled under his breath and returned to work, scraping the chipping old paint off the window trim of one of the cottages. He'd spent the morning clearing brush and trimming vines. A heavy-duty raking and mowing was needed, but already the place looked neater. The white pines that surrounded the area were constantly dropping twigs, cones and needles, so the grounds would never be manicured. That was the charm of the place, but it went against his penchant for order.

"Hey, Howie. Want a job?"

The boy's head jerked up. "Yes, sir!"

Howie had tired of cartoons and reruns of sitcoms.

He'd been hanging with Jake all afternoon, doing his best not to get in the way except for a constant stream of questions. Jake had finally put him to work, hauling brush and scraping the trim.

"Soon as I mow, I want you to rake the grass around the cabins every morning."

Howie considered. "What's the wage?"

Jake swiped the side of his hand beneath the bandanna he'd wound tight to use as a headband. "Fifteen bucks a week."

"Wow." Howie adjusted his backward baseball cap. "I'll do it."

"You're hired." Jake went over and shook the boy's hand.

Kristen hugged her stuffed animal. "I want a job."

Jake studied her. Little girls were an alien species, but even he could see this one was a cutie pie. She looked a lot like Lia, with her pale blond hair caught up in a ponytail and her big blue eyes staring at him through the wisps that had come free. "I'll give you a penny for every pinecone you collect."

Kristen looked at the cones scattered everywhere and her eyes got even bigger.

"Hold out for a dime," Howie advised.

"A nickel," Jake said. Kristen could put him in the poorhouse at that rate, but he expected her to quit long before then.

Howie nodded solemnly. "That's a good compromise, sir."

Jake held back his smile. "This isn't the Army, Howie. You can call me Jake."

"My dad likes to be called sir."

"It's a respectful way to address your elders. But we know each other well enough for you to call me Jake."

"Yes, sir, Jake."

"Sir Jake, huh?" The irony was not lost on Jake, seeing that Lia had made it clear. She might need to be rescued, at least in his estimation, but she did not want a knight in shining armor. So be it. He'd jumped the gun on that whole deal anyway, even if it had been only in his mind.

The little girl tugged at his hand. She held up her bedraggled, lop-eared rabbit. "Cuddlebunny has something for you, Mr. Jake."

Jake squatted. A large pinecone sat between the stuffed animal's paws, leaking sap onto the pink fur. He plucked out the cone. A six-incher. "That's a fine one. Might even be worth a dime."

"We settled on a nickel," Howie said, scraping the sill with renewed vigor.

"So we did." Jake looked at Kristen's expectant face. She had a few pale freckles on her nose and ketchup residue at the corners of her mouth. He'd made them hot dogs for lunch. "Looks like I owe Cuddlebunny a nickel." He stood and searched his pockets. Empty. "Will she wait for her wages?"

"Only if you shake on it." Kristen waggled the rabbit's paw.

Jake stuck the paint scraper inside his waistband. Feeling slightly foolish, he went down on his heels again and took the paw between two fingers. "Deal."

Kristen giggled and stuck out her hand. "Shake me, too."

He heard the grinding motor of Lia's car as she made the turn from Blackbear Road. The little girl's fingers were as spindly and fragile as birch twigs.

She put the rabbit up near his face. "Cuddlebunny wants to rub noses."

Jake gave the stuffed toy a quick rub, then yanked away so fast he almost went over on his butt. Lia beeped the horn as she pulled in, gaining the youngsters' attention, much to his relief. By the time she'd climbed out of the car and dealt with their immediate questions, he was fully in hand, telling himself that he wasn't still entertaining half-baked ideas about setting their family to rights.

"Oh, dear," Lia said, looking at Jake. "The children have been bothering you when I told them not to."

She was in bare feet. Her blouse was wrinkled and stained, and her hair was a mess. But the creased, worried expression she'd been wearing since they'd met was less evident. If she smiled, she'd look more like Sam's older sister than mother.

Jake noticed Howie's anxious eyes. "No, they haven't been bothering me," he said.

"I can tell by your face."

"What do you mean?" He must look funny. Would

she laugh if he blamed it on the encounter with Cuddlebunny, when really it was holding Kristen's hand that had pierced his thick skin?

Lia reached out with one finger. It flicked against the side of his nose like a butterfly. "This," she said, holding out the finger. A tuft of pink fuzz clung to the tip. "Evidence of close encounters with a stuffed animal."

Her lips puckered. With a small puff, she blew the fuzz away.

Jake watched it float on a breeze. He cleared his throat. "Preferable to skunk."

"Yes, thank goodness, this time I'm the only one who needs an immediate bath." Oblivious to his discomfort, she plucked at her blouse where it stuck to her skin. The edge of her bra was outlined beneath the fabric. Why Jake noticed that when he'd been in strip clubs from Fort Benning to Hong Kong was beyond him.

"I feel as if I've rolled in a puddle of melted ice cream," Lia continued, and he tried not to think of her stripped down to creamy bare skin.

"Did you bring us any 'scream?" Kristen asked. To Jake she said, "My favorite flavor is chocolate."

Lia tucked a strand of hair behind her daughter's ear. "No ice cream this time, honey. Where's Sam?" She turned to Jake, frowning. "I know I was gone longer than I'd planned, but I hope she didn't dump the kids on you and take off."

He decided not to mention finding the two youngest

playing "Peter Cottontail" in the garden, especially since that had entailed Howie hoisting Kristen's rabbit on the tines of a pitchfork while she shrieked and rattled the wire gate he'd closed on her. Sam had showed up a few minutes later, saying she'd only gone on a walk, so what was the big, hairy deal?

"She's around here somewhere."

"Uh-huh." Lia sighed. "Other people say she's a great babysitter for their kids."

"She's young." Jake didn't know why he was defending her.

"Right. But she's always telling me she's old enough."

"You don't believe what she tells you, do you?"

Lia smiled crookedly. "Hardly ever."

Jake pulled off the bandanna and wiped at the sweat trickling down the back of his neck. Lia was wrong about the bath. He needed one, too. Considering the way his libido had taken control of his head, a cold plunge into the river seemed about right. "So, aside from the drippy ice cream, how did it go?"

"It was a job. Mindless, hot, sticky. Fortunately the pay's really fantastic." She rolled her eyes. "Minimum wage. But it'll do for now."

Jake tamped down offers of sympathy. She wasn't asking for those, either.

"Mom, we got jobs, too," Kristen said. "Me and Howie."

"You did? My gosh. I hope you're earning a big salary."

Kristen squinted. "What's a celery?"

"Are you being paid?"

"Mr. Jake said I get a nickel for every pine cone I pick up."

Howie hitched up his shorts. "And I'm gonna rake the grass. I get the salary."

"You do?" Lia raised her eyebrows at Jake. "I'll be discussing that with Mr. Robbin, if you don't mind."

"But we made deals," Howie said. "We shook on it. Men don't go back on their handshake, Mom."

"Girls, too," Kristen said.

"That's fine," Lia said. "We'll talk about this later."

Howie's lip quivered. "But—"

"Later."

"Sorry, guys," Jake said. "I should have asked your mom first. She's the sergeant of this outfit."

Howie's glasses glinted. "My dad's the boss."

Kristen was following the conversation with a puzzled, almost worried frown that made her look even more like Lia. "Uh-uh. Mom is." She reached for her mother's hand. "Mom's the boss."

Lia briefly closed her eyes. "Let's talk about this later, please. Right now I can't think straight."

"You go have a shower," Jake said. "I'll look after these two."

"You've already done too much."

"Don't protest. Go cool off. You're not thinking straight."

Lia sent him a grateful look.

The screen door to their cottage banged open, and Sam sprang out, coltish in ripped jeans and an abbreviated top that showed her ribs. She stood on the path and stared at Lia with the full force of her teenage temperament. "Gawd, Mom! How could you do this to me? Working at the ice cream stand is about the most embarrassing thing I can imagine. It'd only be worse if you were a lunch lady at school, and you'll probably do that in the fall so I can be really humiliated. Thanks, Mom, thanks a lot!"

Sam spun in a flailing circle as if she didn't know where to go, then slammed back into the cottage, rattling the door on its rusty hinges.

Lia put a hand to her head. She caught Jake's glower and offered a weak smile. "She's a teenager."

That explanation only went so far, in his opinion. He was itching to teach Sam a few lessons about respect and discipline, lessons he'd learned the hard way in the military when his own parents had failed him.

But it wasn't his place. According to Lia, it never would be.

Unless he took her down the path of the Jake Robbin brand of straight thinking.

"Sam, come outside. I'd like to talk to you."

Samantha was sprawled on one of the beds, her head hanging over the side while she painted her nails blue. She looked at Lia upside down. "Outside? In the godforsaken jungle? I'm fresh meat. The mosquitoes will eat me alive."

"You'll survive. I have insect spray."

Sam didn't move except to cap the polish and let her arms flop free, fingers spread.

"This is a command performance, Samantha, not an invitation."

Her daughter expelled a deep sigh and reluctantly rolled out of bed. "Jeesh. All right, already."

"I don't want to hear another word of complaint." Lia wheeled around, bypassing Kristen and Howie, who were playing a game of Hungry Hungry Hippos on the rag rug. After her shower, the kids had helped unpack the rest of their belongings to make the cottage feel more like home. They'd brought along a small thirteen-inch TV, but there was no cable in the cottage. Only two channels were available, with spotty reception. The kids were appalled, but Lia was secretly thrilled. She'd encourage outdoor activities, something they'd had too little of in their old neighborhood, where she'd been reluctant to let them out of her sight.

She'd had great intentions of keeping the family away from Jake for the night, to give him a break. But cooking in the cottage was limited, and they'd ended up back at the barbecue grill for chicken and roast potatoes. She'd put together the vegetables in his kitchen, then handled the cleanup despite his offers to help, swearing to herself that tomorrow they'd be on their own. She had to stop relying on Jake.

"Want me to spray you?" Lia asked Sam once they were outside.

"I guess."

Lia squirted the insecticide over her daughter's gangly limbs. Sam was already five-six, a full inch taller than her mother, which seemed impossible when Lia remembered bringing her home as an infant. A lot had happened between then and now, including the ruination of all her hopes for the future.

"Cover your eyes." She flipped aside Sam's ponytail to get her neck. "Your shoulders look a little red. Remember to put on sunscreen whenever you go outside."

Sam twitched her bony shoulders. "You're such a mom."

"You're such a daughter." Lia sprayed herself. She'd put on her last clean pair of shorts and T-shirt after her shower. The shirt was old, faded and too tight. Jake had noticed. Tomorrow she'd look for a Laundromat.

"You know, they call it 'bug dope' up here. Isn't that funny?"

"The insect spray?" Lia set the can on the doorstep. "Where'd you hear that?"

"Jake must have said."

"So you did talk to him. The report I got was that you spent most of the day in the cottage. Let's walk a little ways into the woods." Lia resisted taking Sam's hand the way she used to. Sam could still be affectionate, but she chose her own moments.

Sam crossed her arms and assumed a pouty look. "He probably told you I went for a walk."

"No, he didn't mention that."

Sam shot Lia a look from the corners of her eyes. "Well, I did. Down by the river."

Lia's stomach muscles tightened. "Samantha, there's a reason I forbade that. I know you're old enough and can swim, but think about what might happen if Kristen or Howie had followed you."

"They didn't."

"But they could have." Lia cut short the harangue that threatened to spew forth. "A swift river can be dangerous even for a good swimmer. Jake says the current slows farther along. Maybe on my day off we can all go swimming. Until then, promise me you won't go near the water without one of us knowing."

"Yeah, sure." Sam's chin drooped to her chest. "One of us," she muttered.

"Whether or not I want to, for now I have to rely on Jake's help." Lia touched Sam's elbow. "The same way I have to rely on you."

Sam swung her arms away. "Free babysitting all summer," she said with a moan.

"I know it's a lot to ask of you." Lia put her arm around Sam's shoulders and gave her a squeeze. "Give me a few months to figure things out. Life will get better."

"Not if you keep working at an ice cream stand."

"What's so bad about an ice cream stand?"

"Moms don't work there."

"This one does." Lia stopped and looked up at the treetops. Clusters of pinecones clung to the underside of the branches. She smiled to think of Kristen's excitement about the nickels she'd be collecting from Jake. "Do you think I wouldn't have preferred a better-paying job, something clean and indoors and air-conditioned? I tried, Sam. And maybe a more appropriate job will come along. But we needed money for groceries right now."

Sam's shoulders hitched. "I know. I'm sorry I was so mean about it."

"You were rude and you did it in front of Jake. I felt humiliated." Lia pulled Sam closer. "You know what that feels like, right? I do things that humiliate you all the time."

"Not that much." Sam bumped their heads. "You're a kinda good mom. I really am sorry. Just don't expect me to hang out at the ice cream stand."

"Not even for free ice cream?"

"Maybe one cone. If you act like you don't know me."

Lia laughed. "About the babysitting… I know you understand why I can't pay you right now except for a small allowance. I made a deal with Jake for the cottage, but I still need every penny I earn." She stroked Sam's cheek. "Thank you for helping out. I really need you to be dependable right now."

Sam nodded, unusually subdued. "Okay."

"Do you have any concerns?"

"When can we get our own house?"

"Maybe by the end of the summer."

Sam pulled away. They'd been following a meandering path through the woods and had passed two more of the shadowed storybook cottages with steep shingle roofs gone green with moss. The tranquility was what Lia had wished to find, but she hadn't bargained for the total isolation. Total except for Jake.

As if she'd read Lia's thoughts, Sam stopped and turned. She clutched her elbows. "I don't like being alone here. What if Dad finds us?"

"He won't. He has no idea where we are."

Sam's voice rose. "The cops might be looking for us already."

"I don't think so, honey. Your dad won't go to the police, not right away. We haven't even missed a visitation yet." Larry was more the type to hire a P.I., then take matters into his own hands when it came to retribution. Lia was the one who'd tried to work through official channels. Tried and tried until she'd given up and made a final irrevocable getaway.

"What if you get arrested? We'd have to live with Dad."

"I won't let that happen."

"Promise?"

Lia hesitated too long. She couldn't promise.

"At least it would be better than living here." Sam flung the words like darts before flouncing away.

Lia was stung even though she knew Sam didn't mean it. Like any kid dealing with the turmoil of divorce, there'd been times when she'd played her parents against each other, even using the threat that she'd go live with Larry. Hollow threats, Lia had believed, although simply the making of them tied her stomach into knots.

She followed Sam between two tall overhanging pines and found her sitting on the doorstep of a cottage that looked better maintained than the others. "This must be Rose's house."

"It's small." Sam went to peer into a window. "Looks like she moved out already."

"Her wedding presents are at the main house." Lia peeked, too. The interior was shadowed and sparse, furnished with the basics. "Some of her artwork is pinned up."

"I could live here," Sam said, leaning her chin on the windowsill.

"Oh, no, you couldn't."

"But it's horrible sharing a bed with Kristen. And all of us in one cabin. Like we're pioneers or something."

"Maybe we are for now. Blazing a trail to our new life."

"Gawd, Mom. Do you have to be so corny all the time?"

"That's my job—to aggravate you." Lia shoved her hands into her pockets. "Let's go back and check on the little ones."

Sam plopped onto the doorstep. "I'll hang out here." She pulled out her iPod.

Lia nodded. Teenagers needed their space, and Sam certainly wasn't getting much of it lately. "Only for a little while. Don't go any farther and come back before dusk."

Sam inserted the earphones and waited for her mom to go away. Probably gonna see Jake again and hassle him about doing too much for them, which was pretty dumb as far as Sam was concerned. She didn't plan on staying glued to Howie and Kristen every minute of the day.

As soon as her mom was out of sight, Sam pulled out the earphones. She listened. You never knew when your mom might sneak up on you, but it was pretty hard to do that out here because there wasn't any noise—no traffic, no sirens, no people. The most boring place in the world.

Once she was certain no one would see, Sam stood and tried the door. Open. She'd known it would be. They didn't even lock their doors up here. How backward was that?

With one last check for snoops, Sam slipped inside.

LIA PLAYED A GAME OF Hungry Hungry Hippo, then started the children on getting into pajamas and brushing their teeth. She stepped outside, only for a minute, telling herself she was watching for Sam. Except her gaze strayed in the other direction.

The lights were on in Jake's house, but there was no sign of him.

She heard movement among the trees, footsteps. Sam emerged, brushing at her face and hair. She gave Lia an exasperated look. "Were you waiting for me?"

"Just taking in a breath of fresh air."

Sam's eyes narrowed. "If you weren't waiting for me, you were looking for Jake. Do you *like* like him? Ew, Mom. That's so gross."

"Go inside, Sam. Get ready for bed."

"I'm not ten years old."

"Well, you're not sleeping in like a teenager, either. I don't have to go to work until eleven, so I thought we'd do something fun together in the morning." Something free. "Maybe swimming or sightseeing. We could stop in at the library and check out some books." Except that would necessitate showing ID to get a library card. Life on the run had so many complications she hadn't considered.

Agreeable for once, Sam went inside. Lia continued to linger, silently admitting that her daughter had been on target.

She liked Jake. Despite her morning's proclamation against romance. He hadn't offered that, only given her a look, but the idea had been put in her head and now she couldn't get it out.

Aside from the infrequent setup dates and one sorry attempt at a relationship that had crashed and burned the instant the guy tried to take control, she'd been happily without a man since Kristen's birth. Larry had proved that men were more trouble than they were worth, and since she'd been tangled up with him since the age of sixteen, the time on her own had been due. It was a cliché, but she'd needed to find herself.

Four years later, she was still trying. Problem was, thus far she'd found only a stressed-out single mother who was reminded again and again of the mistakes she'd made and the progress she hadn't.

Even so, maybe she was more ready for a relationship than she'd assumed. In a few weeks, when they were settled, when she had a paycheck in her pocket, she'd be closer to equal footing with Jake and she might be...she might feel...otherwise.

Lia raked her hands through her hair. In a few weeks?

Then what was she doing looking for him now?

CHAPTER SIX

JAKE SAT AT THE BAR in the Cedar Swamp, a modest watering hole that had been around so long every inch of wood in the place smelled as if it had been soaked in beer and tobacco. The place was all wood, so the smell was strong. Maple paneling on the walls had darkened with age. The varnished tables, booths and bar stools had been fashioned out of thick slabs of oak, rough-hewn logs and tree trunks. There was a jukebox, a dartboard and a billiards table, but gossip and tall tales were the primary entertainment. Thus far, Jake had managed to avoid the questioning looks tossed his way. He'd met greetings with a bare nod and returned to his beer.

He was brooding.

Earlier, peering between the venetian blinds like a nosy old coot on neighborhood watch, he'd seen Lia cooling her heels outside her cottage. He wouldn't have thought much of it, except that she'd cast several looks toward his house. Lingering looks. He'd almost gone out to meet her, but then Sam had appeared out of the woods and soon they'd returned inside.

He'd grabbed his keys and driven to the Cedar Swamp, then sat outside in his truck for five minutes, debating about going in for a beer. The bar held bad memories. When he was Howie's age, his mother would send him into the bar to look for his father. By the time Jake was sixteen, he was in charge of scraping up what was left of Black Jack after a night of heavy drinking and fistfights. By eighteen, he'd had enough and had gotten out of Dodge.

After that, he'd returned on leave several times and tried to give a hand to his brother and sister, but there was no reaching Gary, and Rose had become prickly and reproachful. In school, at home, on the streets, they were all three considered the wild seed of Black Jack Robbin, destined for no good.

"Another beer?"

Jake shook his head at the bartender. "One's my limit." Drinking to get drunk had never appealed to him.

"Ya ain't got your father's hollow leg," said a squat, rosy-cheeked man one stool over. Sparse strands of white hair looped his jolly face. He was familiar to Jake, but after twenty years away, many faces had lost their names.

"I guess not."

"Black Jack," said the bartender fondly. "Now that man could drink like a fish."

"Like a whale."

Like a shark, Jake thought, *taking bites out of anyone who came near.*

Another man joined in. "Remember the time Black

Jack and Stringbean lined up twenty shots on the bar and raced to the end? Stringbean was on the floor by number seven, so Jack goes and finishes off his own and String's, too."

"It was thirty shots," said the jolly man. Toivo Whitaker, Jake recalled. Owned Bay House with his sister, Emmie, who had all the common sense in the family.

"Black Jack walked out the door, straight as an arrow, started up his truck—"

The bartender leaned in with his elbows on the bar. "Drove down the center line of Main Street—"

"Right through the stop sign and d'rectly into the picture window of Gertrude Marr's penny-candy store." Toivo chortled. "There were licorice whips and root-beer barrels everywhere."

"Gum balls rolling in the street."

"Gert got word and left her bed. She was out there sweeping candy off the street at three in the morning in curlers and a kerchief. She counted 'em up and swore that Black Jack would pay for every piece."

Toivo regarded Jake. "Did he?"

"I don't recall." Jake remembered the incident quite well. He'd been eight. His classmates had started calling his dad the Candyman, after the song. They'd hummed the tune every time Jake went up to the blackboard, till he'd beaten up an instigator after school one day.

The men began another tale of Black Jack's drinking days, involving the rapid consumption of Fireballs. None of them noticed when Jake left his beer and walked to the door.

A woman intercepted him. Old Glory Hallelujah, Gloria Kevanen, who managed to be gaudy and snobby at the same time. He remembered her as being near his sister's age. She used to eye him up behind her boyfriend's back.

"You can't leave already, Jake." Gloria hooked a hand around his arm and pointed to her table of friends. They hooted and waved him over. "Come by and say hi. We haven't seen much of you since you got back to town."

"I've been busy."

"Oh, yeah?" The bosomy blonde cozied up to him. He smelled minty alcohol on her breath. She worked her lashes, trying to flirt. "What's been keeping you so busy?"

"Working on the property."

"You must have been shocked by how run-down your mom's place got. What a shame that Rose didn't keep it up."

"Rose had enough to do."

"Well, sure." Gloria made a distasteful face. "If you count working at the Buck Stop. Ugh."

Jake detached himself. His sister had worked at a roadside convenience store while caring for his mother. Not a prestigious job, but no shame in it either. She had the mettle, like Lia, to do what was necessary for survival. "Where do you work?"

Gloria fluffed her hair. "I don't have to work, but I do hair and nails at the Kute Kut."

Jake shrugged. "See you later."

"Wait!" Gloria ran after him, following him through the door. She pulled at his arm. "How come you're being so disagreeable? Don't you like me?"

He shook her off a second time. "Aren't you married?"

"Off and on." She tittered. "Tonight we're off. If you won't come back inside, maybe you and I can go for a little ride?"

"Nope." He strode to his truck, parked at the curb.

She trotted after him, pouting. "You used to be up for a good time. What happened?"

"My idea of a good time changed." *And I'm choosy about the company I keep.*

"I think the Army turned you into an uptight prig," she said, trying to be sassy. "Someone's got to remind you how to loosen up and have fun."

He got into the truck thinking of Lia and her children. "You might be right."

Gloria reached through the open window and grabbed him by the face. She planted a juicy kiss on his mouth, working her snakelike tongue against his lips to get them to part.

He wrenched away.

"Nice, huh?" She giggled. "Consider it a preview of coming attractions."

"Go home to your husband." Jake rolled up the

window, wiped her spittle from his mouth with the side of one hand and started the truck with the other. Gloria wasn't entirely wrong. There'd been a time he'd have taken her for what she was worth—a few laughs, a lot of drinks, a roll in the hay.

He'd been Black Jack's boy. One of the hot-tempered Robbins. Bad reputation, good for nothing.

Time and distance had changed his perspective. He was strong, capable, in control. And if he had to be good, it wouldn't be for nothing. He'd be good for something—something fine.

EVEN BEFORE THE NOISES began, Lia was wide-awake. Second night in a row. At least this time she had an outside source to blame.

She listened to the sounds in the night. Rustlings in the grass. Sniffles, scratches, a thud.

Jake wasn't home. It was up to her to defend the homestead, like a real pioneer. She slipped out of bed and pulled on jeans beneath her sleep shirt. A flashlight had been tossed in one of the boxes, but she'd never find it in the dark without waking up Howie, who'd been restless. He had bad dreams. They usually surfaced when he was anxious about his father, and he'd been asking about when their next visit to their dad's was scheduled.

Lia rubbed her eyes. *We'll never be safe.*

She cracked the door, half expecting a bear to rise up on its hind legs before her, roaring at her with a hundred sharp teeth. Instead there came a shuffling noise from the bushes near Jake's. She stepped out, staring into the shadows, trying to discern a shape.

Headlights cut through the darkness. Lia shrank back. The gravel and pinecones popped like corn beneath the truck tires as Jake pulled in. His headlights clicked off. The door flew open and he shot from the truck, yelling in a commanding voice she hadn't heard before. "Get outta there!"

Not me, Lia thought as a furry shape scurried off into the woods.

"Aw, shit," Jake said.

She closed the door and stepped down, wrapping her arms around herself. The air was crisp. "What was it?"

"A raccoon. Tipped over the garbage can." The bag had been shredded, and trash was strewn over the freshly cut grass.

"I thought it might be a bear. I came out—"

Jake glanced up from shoveling the trash back into the bag. "To fight the bear?"

She joined him, stooping to help. "Yeah, so maybe I suspected it wasn't a bear."

"You do have to be careful. Could have been a skunk." He flipped over the lid of the can and scooped the corn cob and wad of foil that had been hidden beneath it. "You'll learn. Lesson one is to always secure the garbage can from nocturnal pests."

"Sorry. My fault." She'd sent Sam out with the trash after the dinner cleanup.

"No harm done."

Lia plucked a slimy brown banana peel between two fingers and dropped it into Jake's trash bag. "Yuck. This isn't exactly what I expected of life in the country."

"Not the kind of wildlife you're used to, I suppose."

"Me?" She scoffed. "My idea of a wild time is hosting a birthday party at a water park." Unless going on the lam counted. Which wasn't all that it was cracked up to be when you had to pack up three kids, four suitcases and assorted boxes of junk first. "You're the one with the nightlife."

The angles of Jake's face were accentuated by the moonlight. His eyes gleamed like black water as he studied her. "You keeping a watch out for me?"

"Mothers do that."

He twisted and knotted the plastic bag. "I've already got a mother."

"Of course I only meant—"

He cut her off by clapping the lid onto the aluminum trash can. "Come inside with me."

She almost choked. "What?"

"To wash your hands."

"Um, I really should—"

"Just come." He took her hand, and the jolt to Lia's system must have shorted out her brain, because next thing she knew she was standing at the kitchen sink and Jake was squirting antibacterial soap into her palm. He put down the dispenser. "Wash."

Lia complied. There was no good reason not to.

His hands bumped hers under the stream of water. She withdrew and stood confused for a moment, knowing she wanted a towel but unable to pull her eyes away from Jake to look for one. A dim bulb was on in the adjacent entryway, but he hadn't turned on the overhead light. He looked different in the dark—edgy. Like a slightly dangerous stranger.

Maybe he was.

Jake shut off the water. She was about to wipe her hands on her shirt when he took her by the face and kissed her, his calloused fingers wet and warm on her cheeks.

Lia's breath caught short. The kiss was brief but powerful. He started with firm lips and ended with a soft, lingering withdrawal that pulled pleasure from every inch of her—toes, fingertips, earlobes.

He took his hands away, leaving her standing stock-still, her wet hands suspended in midair, her heels lifted off the floor. She flapped, feeling like a baby bird asking for nourishment. "Why did you do that?"

One corner of his mouth pulled upward. "Because you told me not to."

She rolled her bottom lip. "Did I? I don't remember that."

"Wasn't that the purpose of our talk this morning? Hands off?"

"Then you don't follow rules very well."

"Not unless I want to."

"And with me…you don't?"

"I haven't made up my mind."

"Oh." She scrubbed her hands against her jeans, still tasting him on her lips. "Then why did you kiss me?"

He crossed his arms. "To see if there was anything there."

She didn't need to ask what results he'd found. That much was clear. "But it doesn't matter. I meant what I said. I'm not looking for this."

"Surprise."

"Pardon?"

"The best things in life come when you're not looking for them."

The best things? He couldn't mean he had serious romantic interest in her. She was shopworn, not half as good-looking as she'd once been. Larry had harped on that—how she'd gone from bouncy blond cheerleader to harried hausfrau. He wouldn't accept that it was exhausting to chase after youngsters all day while cleaning house and cooking meals to his standard. Since the divorce, her self-esteem was slowly building but not yet to the degree that she believed Jake found her irresistible.

Still, he had kissed her. Why? Because she was handy, and he was horny coming home from drinking in a bar? Although the overwhelming flavor of the kiss had been all Jake, there'd also been a slight hint of beer. He wasn't drunk. She was sure of that.

"I have to go," she said.

He nodded. "Good night."

She moved away, then stopped. There should have been more to say, but she had no words, only the feel of his mouth on hers. "I have to go," she repeated. "The kids are alone." Now the words came of their own volition, overexplaining. "Howie was restless tonight. He gets these bad dreams, he has a problem with anxiety, my ex was always so tough on him and now Howie craves approval so much he worries himself into a state over every little thing."

She held her tongue between her teeth to stop the flow. "I don't know why I'm telling you this."

"You don't need to, you know." Jake's voice was kindly. "I can see how it is with my own eyes."

She was almost afraid to ask. "What do you see?"

"Everything."

"Not everything." She shook her head. He had no idea.

Okay, maybe some idea. But she doubted he'd guessed that she was a fugitive.

Jake rubbed his jaw. "For one, I see that you need a helping hand."

"Right. Great. Is that what this is, then? You're helping out the charity case and throwing in a little bonus while you're at it?" She swallowed. "Or is the bonus for you?"

The look in his eyes changed as they grew even blacker. His entire body seemed to tense. But his voice stayed calm. "You're way off base. I don't appreciate the suggestion."

Lia fought not to cringe under the force of his emotion. She'd done enough cringing in her life.

At the same time, she had to acknowledge that Jake had reason to be angry with her. Her accusation had been rash. "I'm sorry. I was just trying to figure out why you...did what you did."

"You act like you've never been kissed before." He flexed his fingers. "It was just a kiss, Lia. Kisses happen."

She blew out a breath. "Okay. So can we forget that this one did?"

"Can you?"

"I can try. Because I was serious. I've got enough going on in my life right now without sexual complications."

"I didn't ask for sex."

Not yet. But she couldn't say that. Nor could she look at him. She was out of practice with managing her feelings for a man she might actually like. Or, as Sam would say, *like* like.

"Just a kiss," she said. "That's fine. We'll leave it at that."

It wasn't until she was back in the cottage and climbing into bed that she realized Jake hadn't agreed.

WITH AN EFFORT, LIA managed to remain friendly but distant with Jake over the next couple of days. When they passed, she gave him cheery hellos and kept to polite conversations about her job, the weather, his progress around the property.

There was no preventing Howie and Kristen from their natural attraction to the man. Fortunately he didn't seem bothered by their presence, no more than they were put off by his short answers and gruff demeanor. So that was okay.

Even Sam was being less problematic. She complained about her babysitting duties, but not too strenuously, and joined in when they played board games in the evening. The simplicity and comfort of their togetherness made Lia ache to think that her children hadn't always had what ought to be a given. With a paycheck secured, her children close, the comforting certainty of Jake watching over them from next door, she was almost satisfied.

There was still plenty to worry about. Permanent housing, insurance, dentists, new shoes, school enrollment. To say nothing of the dread always present at the back of her mind. She clung to the completely irrational rationale that nothing too terrible would befall them during the idyllic days of a North Country summer.

On Friday, Lia wasn't scheduled to work the ice cream stand. She promised an afternoon outing to the kids, though first she planned to tackle the cottage housecleaning project.

She put her hair up in a bandanna, then gathered a

mop and broom and other cleaning utensils from Jake's house. He wasn't home. Keeping his distance, maybe, which gave her a pang as she searched the office for keys to the cottages.

The room was tiny and stifling, holding only a desk, a chair and a few other meager furnishings. A metal fan with a cloth-covered cord mended with duct tape sat on top of a file cabinet. The phone was updated to touch-tone with an answering machine that blinked a red zero, but that was about it for modern conveniences. No computer.

Dust and flyspecks coated the window blinds, letting in little light. Two thick stone walls made the space oppressive, especially with the remaining walls hung with old photos, trophy fish and, overlooking it all, the stuffed head of a buck with a large rack. There was a corkboard layered with old coupons and a few yellowed newspaper clippings. On the pass-through ledge where guests checked in, an old-fashioned metal stand held postcards and pamphlets of area attractions.

Lia spun the creaky stand, quirking her mouth at a card that proclaimed the mosquito the state bird. Curious, she flipped open a thick, battered register. Names, dates and comments were scrawled in various colors of ink, going back forty years. The recent check-in dates had grown extremely sparse. Rose had mentioned letting the business die a slow death without regret. Lia wondered if Jake wanted to be here any more than his sister.

The key ring was in the top drawer of the desk. Lia hooked a finger through it, her gaze catching on the framed photos. She moved closer, identifying Rose as a girl and what must obviously be Jake and the other brother, Gary. Happier times—they posed in front of one of the cottages, swimming in the river, building a snowman, roasting marshmallows over a campfire. But there were no pictures of them as teenagers and none of their mother.

The majority of the photos were of men holding up strings of fish or kneeling beside a dead deer or bear, rifles cocked on their hips. One chubby man grinned like a goofball over a fat turkey dangling from its feet. After a minute, Lia recognized a recurring face. The Robbins' father, she surmised. Black Jack, Rose had called him. Always garbed in outdoor gear, he was ruggedly handsome like Jake, with black hair and light eyes that fixed intensely on the camera even as he slung an arm around a fellow hunter or lifted a prize catch.

Rose had rarely spoken of the man except to say that it had been her father who'd run her off when she'd become pregnant. Lia had sympathized, as her own family had been nearly as oppressive about their disapproval and disappointment in the same situation.

Jake looked through the window opening. "What's up?"

Lia dropped the keys. "Oops." She ducked down. "I came to get the keys. I'm going to clean."

"I saw the bucket and stuff." Jake hovered in the doorway, his gaze going to the wall of pictures she'd been examining.

She pointed. "Your father?"

"Yep, that's Black Jack in his heyday. He wasn't camera shy."

"You look like him except for the color of your eyes."

"So they say."

"You don't want to be like him," she guessed.

"Hell, no." Jake's gaze narrowed. "Rose told you about him."

"I know he was difficult."

"That's putting it nicely. He was a great hunting guide and raconteur when he felt like it, but mostly he was a drinker and a brawler. There aren't many photos taken past the late seventies. That's when his drinking got worse and the business began falling off. He kept it—and himself—going for another ten years. After that..," Jake shook his head.

She calculated. "Through your teens."

"I left home. Three or four years later, Rose ran away, and no one knew what the hell my brother was up to." Jake glanced at the photos. "Black Jack was only fifty-six when the drinking caught up to him."

"I remember Rose getting word from a neighbor because your mother was too distraught to get on the phone. She didn't want to come back for the funeral, but she did."

"Rose was the only one of us who got home. I was in some godforsaken shi—dung hole, getting shot at, and it was still better than coming back to bury my father."

"That's sad. I'm sorry."

"For what?" His eyes were dense like charcoal.

She pulled a frame off the wall and handed it to him. "That you don't think of the good times."

She slipped by while he stared at the photo, a river scene showing the kids with beach towels and an immense black inner tube.

He didn't follow. Rather disappointed and not able to deny it, she carted the cleaning supplies to the first cottage and let herself inside. She left the door standing wide and threw open the windows with a screech of warped wood.

The cottage was similar to her own. Not junky but dusty and unused. She fingered a birch-bark lampshade. Thirty minutes and she'd have the place set to rights.

Two hours later, she finished polishing the windows of the third cottage, dumped her bucket of gray water, gathered up the bedding and stepped outside to the sunshine. The scrubbing and sweeping had occupied her, but she'd still thought it was odd that she hadn't been interrupted by any of the kids. They always needed something when she was within shouting distance.

"Scared I'd put them to work," she muttered,

stopping to add another bundle of sheets to her load. Perspiration collected at the small of her back. A cool shower sounded good. Even an ice cream cone, which she'd foresworn after only three shifts of scooping.

She continued to the first cottage she'd cleaned and added more of the bedding onto the wash pile, barely able to see over the mound now as she waddled to the main house, dangling pillowcases and corners of sheets.

No TV, no music, no voices. What were the kids up to?

A small sound made her peek over the laundry. Kristen stood before her, hugging Cuddlebunny, a hand pressed to her mouth. She wore a tropical floral swimsuit and a pair of flip-flops.

"So we're going to the beach," Lia said and then saw Howie and Sam as they circled past the Grudge. Sam had on jeans shorts and a bikini top. Howie wheeled a black inner tube taller than himself. Behind them was Jake with a tube tucked under each arm.

Kristen couldn't contain herself any longer. "Mommy, we're going tubing."

Lia clutched the laundry. She looked at Jake.

He shrugged somewhat sheepishly. "They saw the photo." When she continued to hesitate, he made a motion with his chin. "Good times, you said."

"Well." She hefted the pile, searching her mind for an objection and unable to find one. "I suppose…"

Howie and Kristen burst into cheers.

Sam tried to look bored behind her sunglasses, but she carried a towel and a tube of sunscreen.

Jake caught her eyes. There was a look in them. Gloating, she thought but couldn't see why until he said, "We're ready to go. Why don't you drop that load of laundry and get into a bikini."

Lia's heart sank. There was the objection she'd needed.

"Moms don't wear bikinis," Kristen said.

Jake wasn't hiding his smile. "They don't?" His gaze traveled over Lia even though she was a laundry bag with legs. "What do they wear then? Muumuus?"

Lia gritted her teeth. "They wear one-piece suits with reinforced spandex tummy panels and a built-in bra." To borrow a phrase from Samantha, she'd rather die.

CHAPTER SEVEN

LIA SPUN IN CIRCLES, laughing and shrieking like a little girl. The river current eddied around her, splashing up against the shiny black rubber of her inner tube. When she'd floated free, she let out a whoop and waved to Kristen and Jake, who were following, on approach to the rapids. "Hold on tight, Krissy, baby!"

Jake hugged Kristen to his middle. She was trussed up in a neon life jacket, her tiny hands gripping his forearms. "Don't be scared," he said. "I've got you."

"I'm not scared."

Her trust in him was so complete he was abashed. He had been a protector for two decades, but never to a little girl who'd looked up at him with a sweet smile and insisted on riding with "Mr. Jake."

The current swept their tube into the rapids, which were tame by kayaker standards but just enough to give their group a thrilling ride. Jake let out a yell. Kristen echoed him, then Howie added a shout from up ahead. The boy leaned over the side of his tube and paddled to meet them as they bounced off a submerged rock and spun out of the bubbling water into the wide silken stream.

Lia settled into her tube. "You okay, Kristen?"

"Yeah, Mom."

Jake loosened his hold to dip a hand into the water and propel them in an arc toward Lia. They floated downstream, the tubes gently bumping now and then. Howie wore his like an oversize life preserver, kicking up a froth in an attempt to catch up with Sam, who'd drifted into the lead.

Kristen leaned forward to watch, digging her bony knees and elbows into Jake's legs. "I want my own tube like Howie."

Lia spoke lazily. "You'd fall through, honey."

"Next time we'll get you a small tube of your own. One of the pretty ones with pink and purple stripes." While Lia had been cleaning, Jake had borrowed the tubes from an acquaintance with a pulp truck. The inner tubes were strictly utilitarian, with air nozzles that poked into butts and thighs at inopportune moments. They'd been good enough for the Robbin kids.

Simple pleasures. Good times. Lia had been right about that. Remembering didn't hurt.

She smiled at him from her tube without lifting her head. She was fully relaxed, her hair spread against the black rubber of the tube, her arms and legs sprawled, dipping in and out of the water as they drifted along. She'd appeared in a pair of beat-up tennies and an oversize Lions T-shirt that covered her from neck to midthigh. Presumably hiding a swimsuit. He hadn't expected a bikini but not a linebacker's jersey, either.

She gave a big sigh. "This is wonderful."

Jake grabbed the back of Kristen's life jacket when she leaned over the side of the tube to gaze into the water. He'd told her there were fish and turtles big enough to ride on, and she was determined to spot one. "Hold on there, little one."

Lia lifted her sunglasses, then dropped them without comment. He grinned to himself. She was coming to trust him, too.

"How much farther?" she asked.

"Not far. Quarter mile." He'd prearranged a lunch spot, with his pickup truck parked nearby. His friend had dropped him off at the road with the set of inner tubes, and he'd smiled to see Lia's children running down the driveway to meet him.

These were the times that his idea of the ready-made family didn't seem so absurd, aside from Lia's objections. If he put the argument to her in a reasonable, objective manner, maybe she'd look past her jumpiness about the physical and emotional side and see the many practical benefits.

She cupped a hand around her mouth and used her mother megaphone voice. "Howie. Sam. Don't get too far ahead."

The river was slower and narrower in this section, making a curved pathway of shimmering black and green. Thick trees overhung the grassy banks. A fallen tree stretched along to the left, weathered to silvery gray and spiked with brittle branches like porcupine quills. Sitting on it were two young men, the lines of their fishing poles drifting on the dark water. One of them waved, the other called a hello. Up ahead, Sam raised a hand, then abruptly dropped it and glanced guiltily toward her mother.

Jake watched Lia. She showed no sign that she'd noticed.

They drifted by the fishermen. Jake took a second look, recognizing the dark-haired boy as Rose's son. "Hey, Danny. How are ya?"

The boy did a double take as he walked along the log, reeling in his line so the bobber skimmed across the surface of the river. "Jake?"

Jake gave a shrug and a wave, feeling sort of foolish with his ass plunked in the cold water and Kristen parked between his knees, riding the tube like a horse.

Lia said nothing, but she looked over her shoulder as they floated beyond sight of the two boys. "Who was that?"

"Rose's son. Danny Swanson. Next time, I'll introduce you."

"I didn't know you all were—" She gestured.

"He's been by the house a couple of times, but not since the wedding." Rose had first introduced them the day after Jake had arrived home. She'd been nervous but bursting with pride. The boy seemed like a good kid, from what Jake could tell on short acquaintance. His adoptive parents had done well in raising him. They were supportive of the developing relationship between Danny and Rose and her new husband and stepdaughter.

Which was another good argument for the ready-made family plan. Rose had acquired her family in one fell swoop.

Jake watched Lia. Why couldn't it happen to them?

Lia looked back once more, her face concerned as she idly trailed a hand through the water. Silver ripples followed in her wake.

In a short while, Jake gave a yell and motioned for the older kids to head to shore. They'd reached their take-out point.

"I want to swim," Kristen said once they were close, and Lia nodded approval. Jake set her loose like the pet turtle he'd once turned free in a swamp pond after his dad had kicked over the tin washtub that had been the turtle's home. With churning limbs, she made her way to shore.

Jake slipped off the inner tube and into the water with a small splash. After a moment's hesitation, Lia did the same. She let out a tiny yip as the chilly water enveloped her. "Yikes. It's cold."

"You've been lolling in the sun."

"Lolling? What kind of vocabulary is that for an Army Ranger?"

"I read."

She pushed ahead, spreading her arm outward from the V she'd made with her hands. "You read?"

"*Soldier of Fortune* and *Shadow Warriors,*" he teased. In truth, he'd started reading voraciously during downtimes in the Army. There'd been only so many years-old sitcoms and Armed Forces radio broadcasts he could stomach. He didn't consider himself highly educated except in the school of hard knocks his father had been so fond of, but he was no dumb hick, either.

He pushed one tube and towed the other, feeling with his feet for the pebbly bottom. The older kids had clambered up the riverbank, leaving their tubes drifting toward a patch of cattails.

Lia veered off to retrieve them. "Watch out for bloodsuckers," he warned.

She switched direction, rising with a splash and scrambling for shore, releasing a stream of *ick, ick, icks.*

He admired the wet tee clinging to her curves. The back of the shirt had stuck to her hips, revealing a triangle of blue swimsuit plastered to a rounded behind. "City girls."

So fine.

She glanced back and wrinkled her nose.

After one more look, he went to collect the tubes. By the time he joined them, Lia had unzipped a neoprene pouch she'd brought along and was reapplying sunscreen and bug dope to the kids.

"I'm starving," Howie said. He turned up his face

while his mom removed his glasses and slathered cream on his bright pink nose.

"We have sandwiches." Jake peeled off his tank and spread it over a raspberry thicket to dry in the sun. "Get the cooler out of the truck. It's parked up there, past the trees."

Howie looked at the forest, rife with thick heat and the buzz of insects. "Yes, sir." He marched off in his sneakers and the wet trunks that hung off his skinny frame.

Jake gave him thirty seconds of picking through the thick undergrowth before following. The pickup had been left at the end of a dirt road, a spot known to area fishermen. Two four-wheel ATVs were also parked nearby.

Howie opened the door of the truck. "You take the towels," Jake said. He'd stowed a stack of them on the front seat.

"Nah, I'll carry the cooler." The boy yanked the plastic cooler off the floor of the truck, wobbled under the weight, then put it down to regain his footing.

Jake stood aside. "Can you handle it?"

"I can handle it." Howie hefted the cooler off the ground. It was filled with ice, sandwiches and a six-pack of root beer.

"Good man." Jake gave the boy a pat, got the towels and slammed the door shut. They started back. "We've got to look after the womenfolk."

"Womenfolk." Howie thought that was funny.

Jake pictured Lia bristling. "Don't tell 'em I said that."

"Sure." The boy puffed for breath. "Between you and me. Like my dad."

"What?"

"My dad would say that when he was asking me about Mom. You know, after the divorce. *Between you and me.*" Howie seemed to think this over, and as they emerged from the forest into the riverside clearing, he looked at Jake with a troubled expression. His glasses were flecked with water spots. "I don't know if I should have said anything."

"I won't repeat—" Jake stopped. "You mean you shouldn't have spoken to your dad about your mom?"

Howie sighed. "Yeah. She gets wrinkles when she worries—that's what she says—so I try not to make her worry. But my dad makes her worry. She has to go to court a lot."

"Never mind. You're a good kid." Jake couldn't tell the boy there was nothing to worry about when he doubted that was true. It would be if he knew what he was dealing with, but Lia wasn't talking. He wouldn't pump Howie for information as his father apparently had. That was reprehensible.

They returned to the clearing. Jake decided that not only was this Larry guy an idiot for losing Lia, he was a coward and a sneak. Although the man must have possessed some redeeming qualities since Lia had fallen for him, Jake wasn't making allowances without proof. He tended to be black-and-white in his thinking. A flaw, maybe, but at times also a strength.

He could be a bulldog. Especially when he set his mind on a goal.

Lia greeted them with great cheer that turned out to be more for the beach towels. She wrapped Kristen like a papoose, fussing about how chilly the water was when you were accustomed to swimming in a community pool heated to ninety degrees.

"That pool was gross and polluted," Sam said as she slung a towel around her neck. She'd claimed to be a reluctant participant in the tubing adventure. Jake had kept an eye on her and caught her enjoying herself a couple of times when she forgot to act bored. "Little kids peed in it."

"I didn't," Kristen said, highly insulted. "But Jessica Beverley did and she was in kindergarten."

Howie joined in. "Yeah, well, my friend Tony blew a motorboat fart in it that made all these bubbles—"

"That's enough," Lia said. "Let's have lunch, shall we? Look at the wonderful picnic Jake prepared for us. Wasn't that nice of him?"

"We helped," Kristen said. "I spread the jelly."

Lia knelt beside the cooler and began distributing the food. Jake spread the blanket. Sam asked for the chips. Howie wanted a chicken sandwich without tomato. In minutes, they'd devoured most of the contents of the meal, even the grapes he'd thrown in at the last second for nutritional value.

"Meet the horde of locusts," Lia said, smiling at Jake as he handed her a can of pop.

"That was nothing. Wait till you see what a teenage boy can eat."

"Howie's too skinny." She frowned as she watched him take Kristen by the hand as they waded into the water looking for the minnows that Jake had said would come and nibble on their toes if they stayed still in the shallows. "Sam, too. They get their builds from their father's side of the family."

"You're no heavyweight either."

She plucked at her damp T-shirt. "I still have an extra ten pounds of baby weight. If I don't lose it before Krissy's in kindergarten, I'll have to admit it's not baby weight anymore." Her smile was wry. "A summer in the ice cream stand isn't helping."

"You're fine. Don't worry about it." It bothered Jake when she was so quick to put herself down. He rattled a bag. "Have another potato chip crumb."

"If you insist." She took the bag, tossed back her head and emptied the crumbs into her mouth. She swallowed, watching him sidelong. "Thanks for the picnic and everything. We needed this. I worry about leaving the kids cooped up in the cottage while I'm working."

They weren't as cooped as she believed. He saw no reason to tell her, not right then, but he was torn about whether he should reveal Sam's afternoon "walks." He'd questioned Sam. She'd bristled. He'd told himself to give her some space. All teenagers needed that.

Lia scanned the river. "It's real pretty here."

Jake agreed. "I grew up on the water. Took it for granted until I was stuck in a desert bivouac in Desert Storm. I would have given anything for a dunk in the good old Blackbear River."

Suddenly Sam, who'd been lounging on a towel not far away, sat up very straight. She arranged herself into one position, then another. Lia craned her neck. "It's those boys again."

Jake raised a hand. "Danny. C'mere."

The two teenagers ambled over. Lia looked at them closely while Jake made the introductions. "Lia Howard, Danny Swanson. She's a friend of Rose's. Been staying in one of the cottages at my family's place."

Danny nodded. "Nice to meet you." He was only an inch taller than Sam, with a mop of dark hair that fell into his eyes.

Lia said hello. "We came for the wedding but missed it by a day because of car trouble."

Jake looked at her. She'd said that before, and always so carefully that he had to wonder again what she was hiding. He didn't buy that she'd come only for the wedding and was losing patience with waiting for her to explain.

Lia asked about the wedding, then smiled because Danny wasn't any more descriptive than Jake except to say that it had been nice. He introduced them to his friend, Jeremy Kevanen, a big kid with a happy-go-lucky air. Sam sat tall on her towel, saying nothing but far more alert than she'd been previously.

"This is my daughter, Samantha." Lia waved. "And that's Howie and Kristen Rose, wading. We just had our first tubing experience, but I think we're done for the day."

"The Blackbear goes on for miles," Danny said. His eyes were on Sam. She flicked her ponytail and stuck out her chest.

Lia's eyes narrowed. Mama bear, Jake thought.

"What are you guys doing?" Jeremy called to the little kids. "Fishing?" He took the fishing poles down to the river and they heard him asking what kind of name Howie Howard was. "That'd be like calling me Kevin Kevanen." Howie and Kristen goggled up at the tall young man, not certain if he was making a joke. Minutes later, he had them giggling while he showed them how to cast for fish. "We got to throw back the minnows."

Danny and Sam wandered off together. She was animated, for once.

Lia expelled a breath as she lowered herself to the blanket. "Oh, boy." She lifted her head like a turtle and took another look at her daughter. "How old is Danny?"

"Fifteen, I think. No, must be sixteen." Jake stretched out beside Lia. "He's a good kid. Solid grades, plays on the basketball team."

"That's no comfort. I was sixteen when I met Larry.

He played on the basketball team." She rolled onto her stomach and covered her face with her hands. "Sam's stubborn. She won't listen to me. I can see her heading in the wrong direction, but I can't stop her."

"Maybe if you were stricter."

"Lay down the law? That only makes her all the more determined to rebel."

"She doesn't seem so bad. When I think of the trouble we used to get into…"

"Exactly." Lia rested her chin on her hand, her gaze following Sam as she and Danny walked down to the water. "But I guess mistakes can happen to anyone. I was a straight-A student, belonged to all the right clubs, waved my pom-poms—and still Rose and I wound up in almost the same place."

"Except you got married."

"Like that's an improvement?" Lia made a face, then thought better. "No, it was. Larry worked hard, I got to raise my daughter, eventually we owned our own house."

She told Jake how they'd lived with her in-laws for several years while Larry had gone to school. "I even managed to take a few college courses myself, but then Larry started working and we moved out on our own. He wanted me to stay home with Sam—a sign of his success. Almost right away, Howie came along." She sighed. "I enjoyed being with them full-time, but I still wish I'd stuck with college. Night school, even. I might not have stayed in my marriage as long as I did if I'd had better career options.

"I'm going to drill that into Sam's head no matter how annoying she finds me." Lia rested her head on her arms and went silent.

"College wasn't really an option in my family," Jake said after a while. "My dad would claim that if the school of hard knocks was good enough for him, it was good enough for his kids."

Lia stared. For the past four days she'd barely looked him in the eye. "I have to remind myself that you're retired. You seem too young."

"I put twenty years into the service. Believe me, that was plenty long enough to retire."

Her gaze dropped to his chest and wandered across his arms. "You have a lot of life to live yet. Are you really set on taking over the family business? I get the feeling that your heart's not in it."

"You've been listening to Rose. She's the one who thinks we should sell."

"No, that's not it. We've hardly been in touch for years until recently." Lia considered. "Do you have offers on the property?"

He nodded. "We could sell anytime."

"But you won't?"

"Not while my mother's alive."

"There's something to be said for family tradition."

He cleared his throat. "And for family."

"Are you sentimental?"

"Not in the least. But now that I'm free, I'm rethinking my priorities."

Color had crept in Lia's cheeks. Or maybe she'd simply had too much sun. "Families are complicated."

"Do they have to be?"

"Probably. It's the human condition." She tapped her head. "We think too much. We want too much. And sometimes things get all tangled up and you get to a point where all you want is to be on your own."

Her regret about her marriage showed. Jake touched his hand to the side of her face. Her cheek was warm and soft. Her hair had dried into ringlets that tickled his knuckles. "That's what happened with you?"

She closed her eyes and for a moment seemed to want to brush her cheek against his fingers. He kept them still, and after a hesitation she leaned into his palm. But only for a few seconds before she pulled away.

She turned big eyes on him. "I'm a mother. I'm not on my own."

"Yeah, but put another way, being a single mother means you're even more on your own." He stayed steady. "But you don't have to be." Funny how his voice had come out husky when he was so certain of the validity of his plan. Looking into Lia's eyes seemed to scramble his reasoning.

"I made my choice." She pushed up from the blanket, turning to sit with her legs pulled up to her chin. The kids were all in the water, picking stones to skip, casting for fish. Sunshine struck the surface like diamonds. "On days like this, I can believe that it was a very good choice."

Could be better, Jake said, but only silently. He'd done enough talking for today.

SAM HEARD HER VOICE getting high and squawky like a crow, but she couldn't stop it. Sometimes she swore that even though her mother heard her, she didn't listen to a single word. Or if she did, she didn't understand. She didn't even want to.

"But, Mo-ommm. I'm too old to share a bed with my baby sister."

"I can't help that. We only have two beds." Her mother squeezed a sponge over the sink. "Do you want to switch places? Howie can share with Kristen."

Sam's eyes almost popped out of their sockets. "Then I'd be sharing with you. That's way worse!"

Her mother wiped down their one square foot of countertop and threw the sponge into the dollhouse-size sink. "Well, I'm sorry, Sam, but I don't know what else to do."

"Let me stay in Rose's cabin tonight."

"By yourself? Maybe if it was right next door, but it's the last one on the row, Sam. Too far for me to hear what's going on in there."

"Gawd, Mom. Nothing would be going on. I only want to be alone."

"You're too young."

Too young. That was so stupid. Sam wanted to kick the chair, but she didn't. She held her hands beneath her chin like the little angel her mom wanted her to be and said, "Just one night? Please."

"Absolutely not, and that's the final word."

"That's two words."

Her mother's mouth puckered. Her eyes bulged.

Sam backed away. Yuck. *Is that what I look like when I'm mad?* "Why are you so mean? Dad would let me stay there. He says if I'm old enough to be responsible for babysitting, I'm old enough for other stuff, too. Like a tattoo."

Her mom put her hands on her hips and lowered her voice so Howie and Kristen couldn't hear. "He only tells you that to get to me."

Sam knew that was true. She felt sort of guilty whenever she worked her parents against each other, but all her friends said that was one of the benefits of divorce. Her best friend—used-to-be best friend because now they'd probably never see each other again—had wangled an Abercrombie charge card and a new cell phone out of her dad. Sam was being practically thoughtful asking only for free things.

"I don't care," she said and this time she did stomp her foot. Then she felt bad when Howie looked at her with his googly glasses as if she was a brat or something.

Her mother ran her hands through her hair. No wonder it always looked so messy. She took a breath like she was about to launch into another of her lectures, so Sam grabbed the can of insect spray and wrenched open the screen door. "I'm going outside."

"Don't go far," her mom said, because she always had to give some kind of warning or direction.

Sam rolled her eyes. "Of course not." She tromped up the path, blasting every mosquito that landed on her. Bug dope.

Lights were on in Jake's house. She circled around to see inside his living room. There he was. Big dope.

She'd seen him lying with her mom on the picnic blanket, trying to put the moves on her. That was just so gross. Especially when her mom started looking at him with starry eyes like he was some big, strong hero.

Whatever. It wasn't like Sam thought her mom and dad would ever get back together. Not really. But she sure didn't want Jake for a stepfather. Danny had told her all about his uncle Jake, how he'd been all over the world with the Army and been in wars and stuff, like Danny was all impressed. Sam just figured that was why Jake was such a hard-ass, glaring at her like he wanted to send her off on a ten-mile hike every time she ditched her duties while her mom was at work.

Tough. Sam batted at a moth that was getting tangled in her hair. She sprayed the bug dope into the air, making a cloud of noxious fumes. Probably she would get black lung from breathing in so much poison, but who cared?

Jake came to the window. Crap. He must have heard her.

Sam ducked beneath the windowsill, into a twiggy bush that crunched when she landed on it. She crawled out on her hands and knees. A rock bit into her palm. She picked it up and aimed at the garbage can near the corner of the house. Jake would think it was only raccoons again.

The screen door at the back of the house opened. She held her breath until it closed again and she heard Jake moving around inside.

She exhaled. Something tickled at her ankle, and she slapped it away, then wound her arms around her legs. Gawd. Here she was huddled in the grass, fighting bugs, miserable and alone. Could her life get any worse?

Her mom used to have a cheesy wall hanging that said when life handed you lemons, make margaritas. The only way Sam's life might get any better was if she could figure out a way to sneak out at night to see Danny.

He and Jeremy had said they'd pick her up on Blackbear Road and take her to the drive-in any time she wanted. She couldn't believe they still had drive-in movies here. Like they were living in the 1950s. Or they could go tour-wheeling, which was kind of an uncool country thing to do, but at least it was fast.

All she had to do was get away from her mom. And Jake.

CHAPTER EIGHT

"I'M REALLY SORRY ABOUT this," Sarah Johnson said to Lia. She was chewing on her nails and shooting help-me glances at the girl standing beside her. The interior of the ice cream stand was small under any circumstances, but with three of them squished side by side, it had become claustrophobic.

Maybe that accounted for the tightness in Lia's chest. "Are you firing me?"

"No! I'm only cutting back on your hours."

Sarah might have said something before now. They'd already worked half a shift when the new girl had arrived and put on an apron. "Cutting them by how much?" Lia asked.

"Um, like down to twenty?"

Lia groaned. Twenty hours at minimum wage would barely pay for groceries. She'd have to find another job, which was no easy task. She'd continued scouring the want ads the past week. Aside from the usual work-from-home scams and one request for a live-in for an elderly woman, there was nothing within thirty miles of Alouette. Maybe she could take an out-of-town job as a receptionist or waitress if Jake finished work on her car. The Grudge was already running a lot better. But that would mean leaving the kids for even longer periods of time.

"It's just that Kev broke up with Carly, so she wants her job back," Sarah explained. "And she was here first."

"I dumped him," Carly said around the wad of gum in her mouth. She pushed her bangs out of eyes that were blackened slits from a liberal application of mascara and eyeliner. "He was cheating on me with a ho. Right, Sarah? Jennifer Rankinen is a total ho."

"Uh…right. Sure."

Carly's cell phone rang. She yanked it out of the jeweled case she wore around her neck like a badge and bleated, "Wassup?" Even Lia knew that was played.

Carly began gabbing away as if Lia wasn't standing right there, getting cut back beyond subsistence level. "Yeah, it was such a total drag." Carly let out a squeal. She elbowed Lia out of the way as she turned her back. "And did you see what she was wearing? Omigawd. You could totally see butt crack."

Lia sent a meaningful look at Sarah, who had the sense to seem regretful. "I've been a good worker."

"I know. You're the best. But Carly's my best friend."

"Right." Lia peeled off her apron. "So then I'm done for the day?"

Sarah nodded. "I'm really sorry." She followed Lia to the back door, which was all of three steps away. "Listen. Chances are Carly will cut out on me again, and if she does, I'll give you back the thirty hours. Maybe even thirty-five."

"Sure, let me know." Lia was too dispirited to be optimistic, even though the prospect of Carly's defection seemed likely. "If I haven't found another job, I might be available."

With one more apologetic smile, Sarah gave Lia the handbag she'd hung on the doorknob. There was seventeen dollars in her wallet, all that was left from a cash advance Sarah had given her on the week's wages. Not even enough for a full bag of groceries or a tank of gas. If she ate crow first, her parents would wire money. Only pride had kept her from asking before now.

Lia walked into the parking lot as if sandbags were strapped to her ankles. She checked her watch. Almost three. At least she'd be home early to surprise the kids.

"Tough day at work?" said a young woman Lia had served five minutes before. She sat at one of the tables with her toddler in a stroller, a little girl who was making a mess all over her face with a chocolate cone.

Lia summoned up a droopy smile. "I was just replaced by a sixteen-year-old drama queen with a toe ring and an *I Ching* tattoo on the back of her neck. I bet she doesn't even know what the *I Ching* is."

"I'm not sure I do either." The woman smiled in a curious way. "So you're looking for a job?"

Lia blinked. "Don't tell me you know of one."

"It's only part-time. Used to be my job, but I

decided to stay home with Lucia." She wiped ice cream from her daughter's face. Lucia was a cherub with curly brown hair and a pink rosebud mouth.

Lia didn't dare hope. "Where's the job?"

"The library."

"That must be the one place I missed on my job search."

"It's easy to pass by if you don't know what to look for. Go to Timber Avenue and find the gray Victorian with white and lavender trim. There's a sign outside and a flower garden in the front yard. The library hours are posted, but it's open if you can go right now. Tess hasn't filled the position yet. She's the librarian—Tess Bucek Reed. Supernice lady."

Lia was slightly dazed but nodding. Finally—a stroke of good luck.

"Tell her Beth Trudell sent you."

"Thank you so much. This means a lot to me." Lia stuck out her hand. "I'm Lia Pogue."

"Nice to meet you. I guessed you're new in town. If you're looking for an apartment, I know of one of those, too. A one-bedroom over the Laundromat where my husband and I lived before Lucia came along." She laughed. "Does it say something about my old life that both my job and apartment are still vacant?"

"Oh, no, I'm sure—"

Beth waved her off, still chuckling. "Would you like the landlord's number?"

Lia shook her head. "I have three children. We need

two bedrooms, minimum. We're all staying in a one bedroom now, and my teenager is ready to revolt."

"Goodness. Lucia has so much stuff she's taken over our entire house, and we only moved a couple of months ago. Tell you what. I'll give you a call if I think of a place. I scoured the market when we were buying our house, so I know everything that's available. There aren't a lot of choices if you're planning to stay in Alouette."

Was she? Lia didn't know yet. She'd begun to feel safe from Larry here, but the slim job opportunities were daunting. She couldn't be a part-timer forever, struggling to make ends meet with every paycheck.

The young mother had an expectant look on her face, waiting for Lia's answer.

She shrugged. "I haven't decided."

She looked down at her shirt and jeans, wondering if she was presentable for an interview. Loneliness prompted her to sit down with this nice woman and have a long chat about ordinary things like baby food, muffin recipes and husbands who snored. She'd been missing her female friends.

But she had to go.

"I have to go," she said. "Thanks for the lead on the job."

"It's not much, but I bet Tess will snap you up since you have experience with kids. The summer reading program's big right now." Beth made a funny face to entertain her burbling daughter before addressing Lia again. "What's your number?"

Lia hesitated. "Uh, I don't really have a number right now. I've only been in town for less than a week. We're staying at Maxine's Cottages. You can leave a message for me there."

"No kidding? I didn't know they were still open."

"Rose Robbin's brother is there."

Beth nodded. "That's right. Black Jack Junior. I saw him at the wedding." She raised her brows a little. "Some kind of studly landlord, but I hear he's barely civilized."

"Oh. No. I mean really." Lia's tongue hadn't synched with her brain. Jake was always a flustering subject. She stopped and swallowed. "He's been very good to us."

Beth smiled at Lia, then at her daughter. "Glad to hear it. So you're acquainted with Rose?"

Lia nodded, keeping her mouth shut. The way that everyone in this town knew each other and spread talk like warm butter, she'd rather appear standoffish than give away too much of her past.

Beth continued. "We're having a little gift-opening party for her and Evan when they get back from the honeymoon. Consider yourself invited."

Lia said she appreciated the invitation but remained noncommittal about going. She offered more thanks for Beth's help about the job and hurried to her car. Inside the Berry Dairy stand, Sarah was whirling up a shake and glaring at the back of Carly's head, who was bent over the counter, still talking on her cell.

The Grudge started smoothly. Lia decided that this was turning out to be an okay day after all.

LIA HONKED THE CAR horn as she pulled up outside the cottage, then leaned out the window and yelled, "Pizza!" That ought to raise some interest. There was a storefront pizza joint in town that sold cheapo pies, two for twelve dollars. She'd also purchased a two-liter bottle of pop, leaving her almost flat broke again. That was okay. On Monday she'd get the remainder of her first week's wages from the ice cream stand. The kids deserved a treat.

No one emerged from the cottage. Lia stuck her head inside, dropped off her purse, then carried the pizza cartons around to Jake's house. Voices drifted from the backyard. Howie and Kristen chattering, the occasional rumble of Jake's baritone. Her stomach flipped.

"Pizza," she called, holding the boxes high on her fingertips. "Who wants pizza?"

Howie waved from behind the chicken wire that fenced the garden. "Me!" He held a clump of weeds in soiled hands.

"Me, me, me," Kristen chirped, running over, her plastic beach bucket rattling with pinecones. "My stomach is so hungry it's growling like a bear."

"Hi, sweetie." Lia kissed the top of her daughter's head. "Go inside and wash your hands, both of you." She set the pizza on the table and gave Kristen's bottom a pat to hurry her along. "Jake, will you join us? I have plenty."

He stood and stretched, looking casually sexy in a black tank, faded blue jeans and bare feet. "What's the party?"

"TGIS—Thank God it's Saturday. Plus, I got canned from the Berry Dairy."

"That's good news?"

"Uh-huh, because I found another job. Actually, I'm not canned, only cut back. But between the ice cream stand and the library gig, I'll be making double what I was before. The library pays above minimum wage and they can give me twenty-five hours a week."

Jake came over, squeezed her shoulders and dropped a friendly kiss on her forehead. "Congratulations."

"Thanks." Suddenly she was shy—but also wishing he'd aimed lower. "I got a lucky break. Ran into a woman who used to work in the library, and she told me to apply. I went right over and landed the job through sheer desperation."

"Maybe a little bit of character, too."

"No, it was the desperation. That, and knowing every title in the *Series of Unfortunate Events* books."

Jake flipped open a pizza box. "Don't you need some kind of degree to work in a library?"

"Not as an assistant. Tess—she's the head librarian—said I could take a training class for certification if I want to stick with the job." The kids came out and grabbed for the pizza. She settled them at the patio table and served up slices on a paper napkin. "Wait a minute. Where's Sam?"

Jake squinted. "Uh, in the cottage?"

"Nope." Lia frowned. "She's supposed to be in charge. I told her not to be dumping the kids on you."

He took a wedge of pizza. "I don't mind."

She studied him skeptically. "Come on. There's no way you want to spend your summer babysitting."

Jake shrugged. "A couple hours now and then won't kill me." He winked at Howie, who was watching them with the worried owl eyes while steadily chewing on his sausage pizza.

Lia's jaw gaped. "You're covering for Sam." She turned to Howie. "How often has Sam disappeared?"

He swallowed. "Every day."

"Every day!"

"Settle down," Jake said.

"Don't tell me to settle down." Heat rushed into Lia's face. "You're the one who said I should be strict with her, and now I learn you've been encouraging her irresponsibility."

"Wait a minute. That's not how it is."

"Then tell me how it is."

Jake rubbed his hands against his jeans. He'd been pulling weeds alongside Howie. "I didn't think it was a big deal to let her have some private time. I remember what it's like being the oldest with a brother and sister dogging your heels."

"Arf," Howie said. Kristen giggled.

Lia had to smile. Howie's sense of humor was submerged beneath his anxiety, so it was rare for him to make a joke, especially outside of the family. Jake had made her son feel that comfortable. How could she stay mad at the man?

"Do you know where Sam is, then?"

"Sometimes she goes on a walk, but mostly I think she chills out in Rose's cottage. It's the last one, down there."

"I know," Lia said shortly. "I'll be right back."

She marched off. Maintaining her ire with Sam wasn't easy either when she could sympathize with the teenager's situation. At fourteen, Lia's biggest worries had been her bra size and her unrequited crush on the cutest boy in the freshman class. Sam had dealt with more serious issues.

Lia slowed and snuck a quick peek in the window of the cottage. Sam was sprawled on the bed, writing in the diary her mother wasn't supposed to know about, the iPod plugged into her ears.

Lia opened the door, throwing a square of light across the wide pine floorboards. Sam looked up, blinked and slowly unhooked the earphones. "Oh, boy. I'm busted."

"You certainly are." Lia eased off the anger. "But let's not talk about it right now. Just come with me. We're having dinner over at Jake's."

Sam scrambled off the bed. "One sec." She smoothed wrinkles from the spread, surreptitiously sliding her diary under the pillow. "I thought you were working until eight."

"I got off early." Lia bit back a snappish remark about catching Sam neglecting her duties. Later on, she'd try to impress on Sam the need for following orders and hope like heck that didn't lead to further acts of rebellion.

LATER THAT NIGHT, after pizza and after her mom had launched into a lecture that had accelerated into a bitchfest, Sam lay in bed, faking sleep. The fight replayed in her head until she couldn't stand it anymore. She wished she could put in her earphones to drown the voices out, but then her mother would know she was awake and she might decide they needed a heart-to-heart after their angry words.

That was so Mom. She couldn't just lose her temper and yell and then forget about it. She always had to make up right afterward.

Nothing could make Sam feel right. Nothing except going home, where at least she had some privacy and a phone and cable TV.

She didn't have a boyfriend, though.

Her backpack was on the floor under the bed. Slowly, silently, she reached down and touched the zippered pocket where she'd put the slip of paper with Danny's cell number. Knowing she wouldn't have to be alone gave her the courage to do what she had to do.

Sam rolled to the edge of the mattress and listened. Her mother had finally gone to bed an hour ago. Seemed like ten hours ago, Sam had been waiting so long. But finally she was lightly snoring and that meant she was really sleeping, not just waiting to catch Sam sneaking out.

She scissored her legs out of bed and sat up. The bedsprings creaked. So did the floorboards when she knelt down and slipped into her backpack, pulling the straps up right over her cotton pajamas. Kristen made a small sound and Sam froze, staring at her little sister's face across the rumpled sheet and blanket, willing Kristen not to wake up.

After a minute, Sam breathed again. She'd miss Krissy and even Howie, but at the same time she couldn't wait to get away from them. Her mom…well, she didn't know what to think about her mom.

The key was on the table. Her mom had forced her to hand it over, but then instead of bringing it back to the office, she'd plunked it on the table and forgotten about it. Sam picked it up, uncertain if she should use it or not, except that she was kind of scared about walking through the woods at night. There were no streetlights, not even on Blackbear Road. So maybe she'd go to Rose's cottage until the sun came up. That would still give her enough time to make her getaway.

With one last glance at her mom—and one last twinge of guilt as she whispered goodbye in her head—Sam tiptoed out of the cottage.

KNOCKING WOKE LIA. She was groggy and cotton-mouthed, not ready to get up even though she sensed by the light that it was late morning.

She wanted to bury her head under the pillow, but the knocking persisted. Howie stirred. From the other bed, Kristen bleated, "Mom."

Lia sat up and pushed her hair out of her face. The knocking stopped. Jake, she thought, then looked over to the other bed and saw that Sam wasn't there. Sam slept late any chance she got. They'd had a rousing fight the past night about following rules, and if Sam had gone back to Rose's cottage anyway, there'd be no more messing around. Lia would lay down the law even harder than Jake.

"I'm coming." Lia stood, took a couple of rocky steps, then stopped and looked at Sam's empty spot. Her instincts were popping.

Jake waited outside. "Sorry to wake you," he said, sliding his gaze across her tousled hair, loose shift and bare legs.

The look made her want to wiggle, like Kristen when she had ants in her pants.

"You had a phone call from someone named Sarah. She wants you to work today."

Lia rubbed her eyes. "That was fast."

"I said you'd call her back."

"Thanks for delivering the message. Have you seen Sam this morning?"

"Nope." Jake tilted his head toward the main house.

"No sign of her over there. I've been outside since seven. Wanted to get an early start on the painting." He wore an old T-shirt and jeans with the knees ripped out. A knotted bandanna covered his hair biker-style. His arms were flecked with black paint.

"We had a fight last night, before bedtime. Who knows where she's got to now." Lia suppressed her uneasiness. "I'm probably being punished."

Jake stepped back, clearly intending to stay out of the middle of this one after Lia's snippiness about him covering for Sam. "I'll keep an eye out for her."

Howie appeared at Lia's side. He slid on his glasses. "What's for breakfast?"

"Fruit and yogurt."

Howie disappeared. Jake looked as if he wanted to do the same. "Can I come over and use your phone?" she asked.

"Of course." He gave a short wave and strode away in his square-shouldered, businesslike way.

Lia's toes curled in the sunshine. The sharp scent of the spruce trees cleared her head, and she tipped it back, drawing a deep breath to the bottom of her lungs. The sky was a brilliant blue dotted with the puffy white clouds of a child's drawing.

By ten-thirty she'd made the call to Sarah, fed the children, got them washed and dressed and settled in with books and boxes of raisins and animal crackers so they wouldn't wander over to bother Jake. Sarah wanted Lia to work from eleven to two, when Carly would come back from a vital beach rendezvous with her erstwhile boyfriend. Lia had let the details of the teenage angst float in one ear and out the other. She got enough of that with Sam.

Lia packed up a few essentials—crayons and coloring book, sunscreen, hats, the handheld video game that had been an expensive bribe item from Larry even though his son was more interested in books than animated blips on a screen. There was still no sign of Sam. Lia's concern warred with her irritation. No way she'd ask Jake to look after her kids again.

She gave Howie orders to stay with Kristen and went to stow the bag in the car. Although she remembered leaving the key on the table, a double check of the office confirmed that the passkey to Rose's cottage, number eight, was missing.

Lia had held off going after Sam as long as possible. Her stomach twisted and tightened at the confrontation certain to result when Sam learned that she'd be forced to accompany the family to the ice cream stand. The utter humiliation of that should be punishment enough.

Jake was up on a ladder, painting the trim next door a shiny black. Lia felt him watching, but they didn't exchange words. The man knew when to keep his distance.

She hurried along the forest path. The door was unlocked, but Rose's cottage was empty. Lia stared, uncomprehending, because she'd been so certain that Sam would be there.

Now it was true worry that gnawed at Lia's insides. She ran to Jake without thinking. "Sam's gone. I thought she was hiding out at Rose's place again, but she's not. There was no sign of her there."

Jake climbed down and set aside his paintbrush. "Let me get the keys. I'll check the other cabins."

His steady manner was a comfort to Lia's ruffled nerves. "Okay. I'm going back to my place and see if any of her stuff is missing."

Minutes later, they met outside the main house. Lia read in Jake's expression that he'd found nothing. "Her backpack is gone," she said. "And some of her clothes and makeup but not everything. Do you think she ran away?"

"Something like that."

Lia clenched her hands. "I was sleeping."

He reached out, hesitated, then gave her a stiff hug. "Don't worry. I remember Rose doing this. She'd take off for the entire day, but she'd show up again by nightfall. Sam just needed to get away for a while. She'll be back."

Lia squeezed her eyes shut. They were welling up, damn it. "Do you really think so or are you only saying that to keep me calm?"

Jake looked at her with sympathy, but it wasn't the babying, condescending type of sympathy that Larry used to coax her along with before abruptly getting disgusted with her emotionalism. "I really think so."

Lia checked her watch. *Stay cool. This is just another teenage drama.* "I'm supposed to be at the ice cream stand by eleven."

"Go ahead."

"I can't leave. My daughter is missing."

"I'll look for her. I've got a kayak. I can take that down the river and cover miles before noon. If there's still no sign of her, we'll just sit tight until she comes back."

"What if she doesn't come back?"

"We call the police and report her missing."

A cold dread gripped Lia's bones. "No," she blurted. She saw Jake's puzzled reaction and made a hasty explanation. "I mean, they don't take missing-persons reports for twenty-four hours, right?"

"I think it's different for underage kids."

"I'd rather wait." Lia pressed her knuckles to her mouth, worrying at them with her teeth until she realized she was chewing her skin. "You're probably right. She'll come back soon." A sandpaper chuckle caught in her throat. "Sam's not a nature girl. There's only so much of the outdoors she can withstand."

Lia wouldn't let herself dwell on the thought of Sam walking Blackbear Road during the night, maybe hitching a ride. She'd drilled Sam on that type of danger. The girl might be mad, but she wasn't stupid.

Please, God.

"What about Danny?" Lia asked suddenly. "Sam seemed to know him and that other boy. Jeremy. Do you think…?"

"I'll phone him." Jake went inside, and Lia followed, hovering nervously in the entryway while he made the brief call.

Jake was shaking his head even before he hung up. "Mrs. Swanson said Danny was home this morning as usual, then left for his job at the gas station."

The gas station was a couple of blocks from the Berry Dairy. Stopping there would make Lia late for work, but it would be worth it for the chance to question Danny in person. If he'd had contact with Sam the way Lia suspected, he might have some clue to her whereabouts. Lia would make him tell her.

"Okay," she said, trying to be brusque instead of a basket case. "I'm taking Howie and Kristen with me to the ice cream stand. I'll call you in about an hour—"

"Make it two," Jake said. "I'll check out the hiking trails while I'm at it and stop in at our closest neighbors to see if they might have noticed Sam in the area."

"Thank you." Lia brushed her hand under her nose. "And I'm sorry for causing all this trouble." She blinked rapidly. "We've been nothing but trouble for you, huh? You probably wish you'd sent us on our way that first day."

She didn't wait for his reply, only turned and went to call Howie and Kristen to the car. While she had full confidence in Jake's competence, she still felt as if she was abandoning her post by reporting to work.

Never mind. Bite the bullet and do what you have to do.

Lia had been living by that credo for the past four years. But that didn't make it any easier as she girded herself for a miserable day.

CHAPTER NINE

STEEL-BLUE CLOUDS drifted across the horizon, where the treetops swayed in the cooling breeze rolling off Lake Superior. Jake clicked on the pickup's headlights. Lia had been showing signs of panic as dusk became imminent. He'd left her to make another sweep of area roads.

Lia had questioned Danny earlier that day. He'd admitted that he'd met Sam before, a couple of times along the river. He'd given her his cell number, asked to see her again sometime. But he'd sworn—and Jake had just stopped at his house to press him again—that he hadn't heard from her today. Jake had asked to borrow the phone overnight, hoping that Sam would call now that it was getting dark.

Only fourteen. Alone on the road. Jake's gut tightened.

That she hadn't called Danny was worrisome. Around Lia, Jake kept that opinion to himself even though she'd probably thought of the same thing. She was trying to stay calm for the sake of her other children.

Jake had rashly promised Lia that Sam would be safe, that he'd bring her home. But he'd run out of places to look. If she'd hitched a ride, she might be miles away. Even out of range of Danny's cell phone.

Jake tossed the phone aside. County Road 525 was the main course out of town, a two-lane blacktop road cutting through the dense forest. He'd been down it once already that morning, but he'd turned back at the ten-mile mark. By now, Sam might be stranded much farther away, where homes were few and far between.

Trees crowded the road and narrowed the sky. Sam would feel lost and vulnerable here, one skinny girl all alone.

The phone came to life, lighting up and playing a snippet of a song Jake didn't recognize. He grabbed it and said hello.

"Danny? It's Sam."

Jake braked hard, stopping in the middle of the road. "Where are you?"

"You're not Danny."

"No, it's Jake."

"Jake?" Sam's voice quailed. "What are you—"

"Just tell me where you are, Sam."

Silence.

"I'll pick you up. I'll bring you home."

She erupted. "That's not my home!"

"For now, it is." She wasn't reacting well to his commands, so he tried to soften his voice. "Your home is with your mom."

Sam made a choking sound. "She ran away. I didn't want to." There were tears in her voice. "I'm going back."

"Not on your own, you're not." Lia ran away? He couldn't focus on that now.

"You can't tell me what to do," Sam said.

Headlights popped up in the rearview mirror. Jake eased the truck to the side of the road. "Where are you, Sam? Your mother's worried to death."

"I'm…" She breathed into the phone. "I'm at a pay phone."

"Where?" he demanded. Enough mollycoddling.

"The Buck Stop."

He put the truck in gear and pulled out fast. The back tires spit gravel. The vehicle he'd cut in front of blared its horn. "I'm on my way." He stepped on the accelerator. "Five minutes. Stay on the line. Don't move."

Sam hung up.

LIA SAT ON THE BED IN ROSE'S cottage, holding Sam's diary in her hands and craving a cigarette for the first time in years. She'd never thought she'd be the kind of mother who'd snoop in her daughter's diary, but then, neither did she want to go through another day like today. Her heart had been squeezed into a hard nut in her chest.

She opened to the first page. The words *Samantha Pogue's Journal* were embellished with girlish doodles. Hearts and curlicues. Shooting stars. The diary had been a gift for Sam's twelfth birthday.

Two years of my little girl's life, Lia thought. *Can I do this? Will the diary tell me what I need to know?*

She flipped the page. Several sentences from the middle of the next page leaped out: *Dad says we're living like poor white trash since we moved out. He says it's all Mom's fault. She's selfish.*

Lia slammed the book shut. Was she selfish? Had she put herself above her children? She didn't know. But right now she felt like the worst mother in the world.

"Mom!" Howie's voice broke through her lament of self-loathing. She'd left him and Kristen parked in front of the TV at Jake's, with instructions to yell for her if he called. "Jake's on the phone."

Lia said a quick prayer and slid the diary beneath the pillow, guilty that she'd opened it, grateful that she'd stopped before she'd read too much.

She ran from the cottage. *Good news. Please let him be calling with good news.*

THE BUCK STOP WAS AN Alouette institution, particularly among underage buyers of beer. The place was nothing fancy, just a shack plastered with alcohol and cigarette ads. Hand-lettered notices for rummage sales, free kittens and an out-of-date community pancake breakfast were taped to the window glass.

Jake pulled into the parking lot. Except for a quick stop on his first pass of looking for Sam, he hadn't been into the store since he'd returned to Alouette. It hadn't changed, but at least he had.

There were two parked vehicles—a red Toyota pickup with a barking dog in back and an old junker with several teens huddled beneath a haze of sweet smoke. Jake took a long look inside the car. No sign of Sam.

He went into the store. She stood by the pay phone, holding on to the receiver as if it were a dumbbell, looking scared until she saw Jake. Then she thrust out her chin and smiled flirtatiously at the guy who was looming over her with a six-pack of Bud dangling from one hand.

Jake walked up and glared. "She's fourteen, man."

"Yo, dude." The guy backed off. "No harm done."

Jake ignored him. "Let's go, Sam."

She hoisted her backpack onto one shoulder. "Maybe I don't want to."

"Your mom's waiting."

Sam's bravado crumpled. "Is she mad at me?"

He took the backpack. "Maybe tomorrow. Tonight she'll just be glad to have you back."

Once they were on the road, Sam lapsed into a sullen silence.

Jake was blunt. "Why did you run away?"

She looked out the window.

"Why, Sam?"

"Jeez. I didn't run away. If I ran away, would I be here?"

"Maybe you didn't really want to run away."

"Maybe. Wow, Jake. You're so smart."

He grunted. "And you're a smart mouth."

She put her nose in the air, almost proud. He hadn't meant it as a compliment, but who knew with teenage girls? From her polished toes to her blue-streaked hair, nothing about Sam was black-and-white.

"What did you mean about your mother running away?"

Sam blinked. "I didn't say that."

"Yeah, you did."

"You must have been hearing things." She turned her head and refused to say another word.

LIA HUGGED SAM LONG and hard. She held her at arm's length and looked her over, hugged her again, then said fiercely, "Don't ever do this again."

Sam's eyes had welled up. She rubbed at them, smudging her makeup. "I didn't do anything."

"Uh-huh. Then where were you all day?"

"I hung out. It's not like I wasn't coming back. I just wanted to get away for a while."

"Don't lie to me, Sam. Jake had Danny's cell phone. You weren't calling home."

"I was gonna get a ride from Danny."

"To where?"

"Here."

Lia didn't know what to believe. For now, she was satisfied merely to have Sam standing before her, even if part of her wanted to lock up the girl until her twenty-first birthday. How was she going to get them both through the next several years? The responsibility seemed too big to bear, especially alone.

She held Sam's face between her hands, wishing she could wash off the makeup and take out the piercings and get her happy little girl back. "Have you had dinner?"

"Um, not really. Only some junk food."

"Go to the cottage. There's a sandwich for you in the fridge." Lia had been making them for Howie and Kristen when she'd looked down and realized that she'd put together a third sandwich on autopilot. She'd had to bite her tongue to keep from busting out into tears because Sam wasn't there to eat it.

Sam turned, dragging her backpack. She mumbled.

"What was that?" asked Lia.

Sam sighed. "I'm sorry, okay?"

"I know. I'm sorry, too. I should have been paying more attention to how hard this has been on you."

Lia folded her arms tight against her body while she watched Sam walk away. Her eyes burned. She didn't blink until the cottage door closed.

Jake stepped out of the pickup truck and shut the door with a thunk.

"Thanks," Lia said with tears in her eyes. "Thanks again." She gave a wet laugh. "I can't believe I'm crying."

He came over and looped his arms around her. "You've had a hard day."

She let herself sink into him. Her fingers gripped his

shirt, pulling it into taut wrinkles. She was trying not to put her arms around him, but it was difficult not to. So difficult. She wanted the closeness. The security. But even more, she wanted the desire that would make her feel like a woman instead of a mother, at least for a little while.

Thinking about herself. Selfish.

A sob escaped. Weak.

"What is it?" Jake asked, caressing her hair.

"I've screwed everything up. We're in this terrible situation—basically broke, practically homeless, nowhere to go. I thought I was doing the right thing for the kids in the long run, but now..." She shuddered. "Sam—she's so unhappy. I don't know. She has to be horrendously unhappy, right, to run away?"

All the doubt Lia had been feeling came out in a mournful wail. "I'm a terrible, rotten mother, aren't I?"

Jake moved back a few inches. "Do you really need me to answer that?"

"I don't know."

"C'mere." He took her by the hand and led her into his house. She resisted slightly, thinking that she should be with Sam right now, but he didn't let go. He brought her into the kitchen and filled a glass of water at the sink and gave it to her. Her throat was too tight to drink, but she tried. The cold water eased the ache, and she drank the entire glass, squeezing her eyes shut as she tilted her head back and gulped.

Relief spread through her. There was no reason for

it that she could see. Except that she felt accepted by Jake. He was a solid bulwark in her topsy-turvy world. Dependable and trustworthy. She'd never had that before. It was a terribly seductive thing when she felt so beaten down.

She reached deep for the strength to resist. "I should get back."

"Don't go."

She glanced up at him. "This isn't about me." Or it shouldn't be. Her children had to be the first concern in spite of her moments of weakness.

"That's right. It's about all of you. And maybe I have the solution."

"What are you—no, don't tell me. I have to figure this out on my own. Sorry about crying on your shoulder." Busily she rinsed the water glass several times, put it in the dish drainer, then picked it up and dried it with a linen towel. "I need to go and talk with Sam now."

She straightened her shirt, her thoughts jumbled. Jake's overtures seemed straightforward, yet invariably they ended up confusing her more than ever.

He followed her to the door. "Sam said something that made me curious. About you running away, not her. What did she mean by that?"

Lia stared straight ahead. "I..."

Jake moved ahead of her to put his hand on the latch of the screen door. Brown and white moths beat their wings against the wire mesh. "I've known from the start that you were hiding something. Don't you think it's time you told me?"

"I don't want to get you involved."

"Too late. I'm involved."

Not criminally. She licked her lips and amended her own thoughts. Technically she wasn't a criminal. Yet. Not until tomorrow, when the kids didn't arrive at their father's house for the scheduled visit. That was when Larry would go ballistic and she'd find out how much trouble she was really in.

"We're not involved," she said with a sinking feeling.

Jake snorted. "You're fooling yourself." Typically blunt.

"You don't have to take on my family problems, you know. It's okay to stay detached."

"What if I don't want to be?"

"After all the grief we've given you? That's crazy."

He smiled a little. "You still don't believe that I know my own mind."

"I'm sure you do." She couldn't figure him out, but that was another thing. And she didn't know what he expected from her.

He opened his mouth. "Don't," she blurted.

"Why?"

She realized that she was afraid of what he'd say. Because she might like it too much. And that put them back at square one—if they'd ever left it. She wanted progress, not setbacks.

"Please don't," she said. "It's late and I want to go next door and hug Sam again. I start work at the library tomorrow and I have to figure out what to do with her besides locking her in the Grudge's trunk."

Jake's face was impassive. He opened the door and moved to one side so she could pass. Immediately a moth flew inside, fluttering straight up to the ceiling light. Lia drew in the scent of the wilderness and tried not to think about wanting what would burn her the most.

"I don't give up," Jake said softly behind her once she was past him and standing in the cool grass.

"Well, me neither." Which was true, regardless of her momentary breakdown. If what she'd done was selfish, she'd have to live with the label. Someday Sam would get it. Someday Jake might, as well.

The lonesome sound of the hooting owl stopped her on the doorstep. She waited for a response. Jake's silhouette was framed by the neighboring doorway. He was waiting, too.

They looked across the yard at each other. Lia wanted to fly into his arms. If the owl got an answer…

But it didn't. The owl hooted several times, hauntingly beautiful calls, but there was no reply.

THE LIBRARY JOB WAS bliss. Peaceful, orderly bliss.

Tess Bucek Reed showed Lia around. The main room, with tables and the checkout desk. The rows of nonfiction, leading through an open door into adult fiction. Periodicals and newspapers were lined up against a back wall. "There's a single lavatory off the foyer," Tess said. "My office is right there, too. I don't use it that often during business hours since I'm usually in here, overseeing the patrons."

She *click-clacked* in heels to the front desk. "I'll put you in my office to fill out your paperwork."

Lia clenched. "Paperwork?"

"The usual W-2 and a few other forms we need. I'm sorry we don't offer benefits to part-time workers. I wish we could, but the budget is tight enough as it is. The library board held me off from hiring Beth's replacement as long as possible, but I told them I seriously need the help. I can't run the entire place on my own." While Tess talked, she opened a file drawer and pulled papers from a neatly labeled file. "Especially in the summertime. I run a reading program that gets many participants. We have story hour several times a week—you'll always need to come in at those times—but kids are running in and out all the time."

Tess pointed with the sheaf of forms. "The children's section. Where the action is."

A room that must have once been a front parlor or sitting room was now lined with low bookshelves and decorated with colorful posters, craft projects and hanging plants. The bright tables and chairs were sized for children. Several of them were occupied with youngsters absorbed in their reading. A mother looked up at Lia and smiled.

Tess stood at Lia's side. "You said you have children?"

Lia faced the petite librarian. "Yes. Three of them." She glanced at Tess's wedding ring. "What about you?"

"Gosh, no. I'm still a newlywed. Connor and I were married this past New Year's Eve. Of course, Claire and Noah were married at the same time, and look at the state she's in."

Lia recalled the pregnant woman she'd met in the grocery store, once again reminded that everyone in town seemed to know the business of everybody else. Some only assumed they did, according to Rose, who'd been scarred by such innuendo.

"Back to business," Tess said. "I realize that flexible work hours can be a hassle when there are offspring to consider. Have you been able to find adequate child care?"

"Um, well, my oldest daughter—Samantha—is fourteen. I'm relying on her a lot. And there's an adult nearby who pinch-hits."

"That's right—you're staying at the cottages on Blackbear River. I heard about that." Tess grinned. She had a merry kind of face with keen eyes and a quick smile, framed by short coppery hair. "When I mentioned to Beth that I'd hired you, she filled me in on everything she knew. We agreed that any friend of Rose's is a friend of ours." She lowered her voice a notch. "Don't look so concerned. You get used to the familiarity. Before long, you'll be just another face among the crowd. If the population of Alouette can qualify as a crowd, that is."

"I sure hope so."

Tess smiled warmly. "Follow me." She led the way through the Victorian structure's foyer and into a small office with space for only a desk and an old-fashioned wooden desk chair. "Have a seat. Take a pen. I'll give you time to complete the paperwork and then we can dive right into instructions on library operations."

"All right," Lia said a bit nervously. Learning the routine at the ice cream stand had been a snap because of her experience as a waitress. Library work was brand-new.

"Easy breezy." As she departed, Tess waved airily, making the light catch on her diamond ring.

Lia stared at the tax forms. She'd had a diamond, too. Not an engagement ring, but a seventh-anniversary present. Larry had boasted about its value, then complained bitterly when the ring went to Lia in the property settlement, even though he'd come out of negotiations with almost everything else.

She'd held on to the ring through Howie's tonsillitis and a spell of unemployment. Not out of sentimentality—for backup. But when she'd been laid off from her waitress job the same winter that fuel prices had shot sky-high, she'd finally hocked the ring to keep their apartment heated. Since the divorce, she'd learned that poverty didn't necessarily arrive in one fell swoop.

It crept in, linking one lousy break to another. Every time she'd been able to get ahead of her bills, disaster struck in the form of car repairs or fillings or another challenge in court by Larry and his sharky lawyer.

Bringing me to this. Lia filled in her social security number. There was no other choice. Maybe she'd get lucky for once and Larry would decide that he'd tortured her long enough. He might finally choose to let Lia and the kids go.

Fat chance.

Tess returned minutes later and took a quick glance at the top form. "Lia Howard. Is that your married name? Because Beth thought you were called Pogue."

Lia shot to her feet as if a trigger had been pulled. "Where did she get that idea?"

Tess blinked at Lia's alarm. She didn't miss a trick. "From you, I believe."

"Oh." Lia frowned. Had she slipped up and given the wrong name? Maybe. She'd been stressed about the Berry Dairy cutback at the time. "Howard is my maiden name. I went back to it after the divorce." Only recently, granted, but still true. "Sometimes I forget."

"How long were you married?"

"Eleven years, give or take, counting the separation." Lia didn't want to discuss the divorce, but she hated being rude when Tess had treated her with nothing but kindness.

"Must take some getting used to," Tess said softly, apparently assuming the issue was a fresh wound.

Uncomfortable with the whole thing, Lia said, "It's not a part of my life that I like to talk about."

"Of course." Tess took her by the elbow. "Enough of the chitchat. Let's put you to work."

CHAPTER TEN

"THEY'VE TAKEN ME under their wing," Lia said the next day, not even thirty minutes after the excitement of the arrival of Rose and her new husband, Evan Grant, who were back from their honeymoon and had come to the cottages first thing. "Claire, Beth, Tess. Especially Tess. As soon as she found out that I've always wanted to go back to school, she started running Internet searches for information about scholarship programs for older students. She says it's the librarian in her, but I think it's more out of the goodness of her heart."

"That's Tess," Rose said with a grin. "She's a bundle of energy. She mentored Beth from the day she walked into the library as a girl. And I know she had a hand in Evan and me getting together." Rose smiled fondly. "Not in an annoying busybody way. Tess is too nice for that. She just always manages to find a way to help out at the right moment. Has she roped you into the Scrabble tournament yet?"

"Nope. But I signed up Howie for the children's division."

Rose laughed easily. "He'll win it, too."

"He's making lists of words and wants to play a practice game every night." Lia gazed at Rose in wonder. "So it looks like marriage agrees with you."

"Weird, huh?"

"Not weird. It's nice. I like seeing you this way. But it takes some getting used to. Naturally Kristen didn't remember you, but even Howie didn't recognize you right away."

Rose twisted a strand of hair. "I've changed that much?"

Lia nodded. "Not in looks, particularly. It's hard to define, but it's more in your manner. You're just plain happier, of course, but also, like when you put your head down and your hair fell in your eyes—that was more like the Rose I remembered."

Rose rumpled her dark hair. "I'm still me."

"I know, I know. I'm so thrilled to see you again." Lia had said that only three or four times already.

"Me, too."

"Three years almost." Lia surveyed the river. The scene was idyllic once again. A long way from their old stomping grounds downstate.

They sat in the sun-bleached Adirondack chairs at the top of the slope. Below, Jake and Evan were teaching the kids how to kayak. Kristen and Lucy Grant had become swift friends—two little blond girls holding hands and splashing through the shallow water. Sounds of laughter and happy voices drifted through the gently swaying trees.

Lia sighed. "Now that I'm here, I can see why you decided to stay."

"I stayed out of duty, not for the view," Rose said, but there was no bitterness in her tone. She clunked her head against the high chair back and groaned. "I'm really gonna get an earful from my mother when she finds out that I came to visit you before her."

"Jake hasn't said much about her. How's she doing?"

"Terrible, according to Maxine. Her doctor says that she may be able to come home soon."

"That's good."

Rose pulled a wry smile. "I guess so."

"What will she think of me moving in and all?"

"She'll disapprove at first, but if you take ten minutes a day to listen to her complaints, you'll win her over. Especially if you agree that her life is terribly hard and her children are so neglectful that she deserves to smoke a cigarette even if she'll blow up her oxygen tank in the process."

"Yeesh. I better find a place of my own real fast."

Rose sipped from a can of cherry-limeade soft drink. "No, seriously, take your time. Having your family around is a good influence on Jake. He's been alone so long I would've never expected him to get along with your kids so well, so fast." She pointed. "But look at that."

Lia looked. Jake was in the water up to his chest, flipping Howie off his shoulders with a great splash.

Kristen and Lucy squealed with delight, clamoring for their turn.

"He could be a family man yet," Rose mused. "Well, why not? It happened to me, it can happen to Jake. And you, too."

Lia resisted. She had to resist. If she didn't, she'd fall into the old pattern of dependence. "Don't get ideas."

"Why not?" Rose lifted her brows. "You can't still be the reluctant nun."

"Not exactly. I simply have other priorities right now."

"But there is something between you two. I could see that after five minutes. Plain as day."

"I won't deny he's attractive—if you like authoritative men." Except that he'd been gentle with her, Lia realized. For the most part, very gentle, very considerate.

"And you've had enough of that type?" Rose guessed.

Lia contemplated. "Not the way you'd think. Larry wasn't only bossy. He was sneaky, too. He undermined my confidence a lot. Meaning I don't feel capable of standing up to Jake the way his ideal mate should. He's a strong character."

"He had to be. The day after his eighteenth birthday, he left for the Army. But first he confronted Black Jack and put the fear of the devil in him about how he'd better treat me and my mom right while Jake was gone.

It worked…for a while." After a moment of melancholy, Rose cast the mood aside. The woman Lia had known would have sunk into dourness.

"Back to you and Jake," Rose said. "You're really not interested in hooking up?"

Although Lia's admiration for Jake continued to grow, she shook her head.

"Oh, come on, woman! Let's look at the facts. Jake's single with an Army pension and he has no terrible habits except being so opinionated. Granted, he went overboard with the tattoos. And he does get really dirty and sweaty, but at least he showers every day." Rose chuckled. "He has muscles on top of muscles. He's even got all his hair now that the buzz cut has grown out. That puts him leagues above every other man you've dated since the divorce."

"In retrospect," Lia replied, "they weren't all that bad." No man had been Mr. Right because she hadn't been in a place where relationships seemed viable. She wasn't convinced that she was there now, either. Despite Jake's many fine qualities.

Rose scratched her wrist. "Larry still doing a number on your head?"

Lia knew she could confess to Rose about how and why she'd fled her husband's reach. Telling everything would be a huge relief. But not today.

"After the divorce was final and I got the restraining order to keep him at bay, he sort of ran out of ways to wreck my life. The only tie left between us is the kids." She shrugged as if the threats to take them away from her weren't deadly serious. "So he uses them to get to me. That's why Sam came home with a lip piercing and Howie gets so stressed. Larry would practically interrogate the poor kid about every detail of our lives. Kristen's still too young to realize the games he plays, but he'd have gotten to her, too, if I'd stayed."

Rose's eyes narrowed. "Larry must be really frustrated that you've moved so far away."

Lia fixed her gaze on the river. "Yes, that's a problem." She let the silence grow, biting her lip to keep from saying more.

Rose became regretful. "I wish I'd asked you to move north years ago instead of losing touch the way we did."

"I don't know if I would have. It's like an alcoholic hitting rock bottom. I had to be ready for the change." And pushed beyond the brink of reason.

"How's the adjustment to your new life going?"

"Rocky," Lia admitted. "Sam ran away. But Jake got her back."

Rose pulled a barrette from the pocket of her shorts and scooped her hair into it. "She reminds me of me. All that turbulent teenage angst."

Lia squinted into the sun. Sam was in the kayak. She'd pouted when Jake had made her put on a life jacket, but she appeared to be enjoying herself now, paddling back and forth under his direction. "She has the prettiest smile when she forgets to be moody."

Rose leaned forward in the chair, putting her chin in her hand as she squinted at the shining water. "Let's go join the fun."

"You just want to get some loving from Evan," Lia teased. "It's been all of ten minutes."

"Fifteen," Rose said with a laugh as she stood. She loped down the hillside.

Lia followed more slowly. She wanted to savor the sight of her children being children without a care in the world.

Jake's doing.

Hmm. Why was she resisting again?

For some reason, he seemed to be attracted to her in spite of her bedraggled appearance and the body that had gone soft and a little lumpy after the birth of her children.

She thought of Rose's story about the young man trying to protect his mother and sister even while he was gone. *I arouse his sense of honor and duty,* she decided. *He only wants to take care of us.*

No basis for romance.

But it's not even a romance, she mentally revised. He hadn't offered that, outside of one wowzer of a kiss. He felt sympathy. He was sorry for her and the kids and he'd taken them on as a project, like tending the garden or fixing up the cottages.

And yet...

Kristen ran up to Lia chattering a mile a minute, just about leaping out of her skin. Lia lifted her girl into her arms, hugging the hot, skinny body close, inhaling the scent of sunshine, bug dope and river water.

Evan and Rose had their arms around each other. Jake looked over at Lia. She flushed when he smiled with a crook of one eyebrow. He was shirtless and gleaming wet. Rose was right—muscles on top of bronzed muscles.

And yet…

"Put me down, Mom," Kristen said, and Lia lowered her wriggling child. She splashed through the shallow lapping water, heading straight for Jake.

Howie and Kristen love him. Sam tolerates him. We're better off with him than we were alone.

He's right in so many ways.

Lia shut her eyes to the seductive scene. *And yet I can't do it.*

FRIDAY EVENING WAS the get-together at Bay House for Rose and Evan to open their wedding presents with a group of friends. Lia had been told that the affair was casual. Everyone, including her offspring, was invited.

Jake had another idea.

"This is your babysitter," he announced at the door to the cottage, waving at the young woman who'd driven up in a lime-green VW Bug. "Her name is Mary Ann, she's a vegan and a massage therapist, and Evan Grant recommended her."

"You consulted with Evan over babysitters?" Lia smirked at the picture. Evan wasn't as rough-and-tumble as Jake, but he was the vigorously athletic type, a teacher at the local high school who coached basketball.

"A man's gotta do what a man's gotta do." Jake rested his hands on his hips. He was freshly shaved and dressed up as much as she'd ever seen—in dark blue jeans and an Old Navy pullover with a zipper and red stitching. She couldn't imagine him shopping in a mall.

"My treat," he added. "Because if I have to go and watch women squeal over wedding gifts, then I'm going to make an evening of it and take you out to dinner afterward."

A date. Warmth rushed into Lia's face, followed immediately by a cold tingle that crept over her scalp from her nape. She opened her mouth.

"No objections," Jake said in his commanding-officer voice.

"Yeah? What if *I* object?"

Jake looked evenly at Sam over Lia's shoulder. "You're underage. You have no say."

Sam bristled with irritation. "I will not have a babysitter!"

Lia didn't get a chance to step in. Jake said, "Yes, you will. You haven't proved yourself reliable."

Sam glared. "I watch the kids every freakin' day."

"Except when you run off."

"One time," she snapped. "One mistake. Can't I make one mistake without—"

"Wait a minute." Lia raised a hand, hushing both of them. "I don't want to listen to an argument. Jake, I thank you for the babysitter. Sam, you have been cooperative since your so-called mistake. Therefore you deserve a break. So the babysitter will be for Howie and Kristen." Both of whom were pushing into the crowded doorway, trying to get a look at the woman, who had round blue sunglasses and white-girl dreadlocks that fell to her waist. "And you, Sam, will come with us to Bay House."

While Jake's expression didn't change, Lia sensed his dismay. She was quite proud of her neat solution for truncating the date.

Sam was intent on being disagreeable. "I don't want to go with you guys."

"Danny will be there."

Lia took her daughter's resulting silence for compliance. Jake's, too.

"Are we ready?" She got her bag from the bedroom, stopping to take a quick look in the mirror. Eye makeup emphasized their color, but her hair hung like a dishrag. Well, she'd done her best. "Ready, Sam?"

"Guess so." She slumped and clumped her way toward the door.

Lia chatted with the babysitter about rules, snacks and bedtimes, then climbed into the high seat of the truck with Jake holding the door and offering her a hand. Her nerve endings fried, even after he let go.

Particularly when he leaned in to whisper in her ear. "It's still a date."

BAY HOUSE WAS A LARGE red sandstone home built in a Victorian style at the turn of the previous century. The building qualified as a small mansion, Jake supposed, watching Lia be impressed by the opulence of a turret and a bay window, copper roofing, a wraparound porch.

"Wow," she said. "I didn't realize they had homes like this in Alouette."

"A few. This is the ritzy neighborhood." They'd driven up Bay Road into an area of thick forest broken by long driveways that wended through well-tended grounds. "I always lived on the wrong side of the river."

"Doesn't seem wrong to me."

He nodded. "Anyway, wait till you see the view from the back garden. We're on a cliff that overlooks Lake Superior."

"Bride's Leap," Sam said unexpectedly. She sat between them, a silent, grumpy chaperone.

"What are you talking about?" Lia asked.

"Uh, Danny told me. It's a legend."

"She's right." Jake parked the pickup along the edge of the driveway. There was a nice graveled parking area, but it was already filled. "Some ancient relative of the Whitakers was supposed to have jumped off the cliff when she was jilted on her wedding day." He left Sam to add her two cents while he got out and circled to the passenger side.

"What a cheery story." Lia looked into Jake's eyes as he gave her his hand out of the truck. He was feeling kind of slammed ever since she'd appeared at the cottage door, glamorous in makeup and high heels. She could look classy when she wanted to. Maybe too classy for the likes of the son of Black Jack Robbin.

He gave his hand to Sam. She showed surprise at the gesture, but she took his hand and hopped lightly from the running board with a swish of her hair. She'd doused herself with perfume and had on more jewelry and eye makeup than he'd allow any child of his. In Jake's opinion, Lia gave in to her daughter too often.

She seemed apprehensive as they approached the front door. "Tess said this was a casual party."

"I'm sure it is. You'll understand after you meet the Whitakers. They're regular folks who just happen to have a mansion in the family."

"It's a B and B, Mom. What's the big deal?"

"No big deal," Lia agreed.

Jake squeezed the back of her neck as Tess opened the door and welcomed them to the gathering. Lia had no reason to worry about fitting in. No reason that he understood, anyhow. One of these days he'd get her figured out.

As the party progressed, he found himself watching her a lot. She was quiet at first, sticking to one stiff brocade chair in the parlor even though the other guests drifted from room to room and out to the garden, where Sam had parked herself at a table with Danny and someone's tail-wagging golden retriever. Between Tess and Claire and Emmie Whitaker—the round and dimpled steamroller who owned the house with her brother Toivo—Lia was soon introduced, chatted up and handed a full plate of food from the buffet.

Hearty home cooking. Jake looked over the dinner table loaded with dozens of hot dishes and salads. He should have known. Laying out a fine meal was a point of pride with Emmie Whitaker and her Finnish housewife cronies. They guarded family recipes like gold and constantly strove—in an unspoken but cutthroat competition—to produce the ultimate pie crust. His own mother had been renowned for her rhubarb pie.

He ate a chunk of Finnish squeaky cheese, then went for a slice of the pie-plate pasty. Tasted like home.

"Eat up, boys," Emmie said, standing at the head of the table with her hands tucked under her apron. She zeroed in on Jake. "You, with the hungry eyes. Make a dent in that rice pudding over there."

"Good stuff," someone said.

"Beats K rations," Jake added as he reloaded a plate.

"I should hope so." Emmie gave him a roll and took the empty basket to be replenished in the kitchen.

Jake's comment prompted a discussion about war and politics that never quite got off the ground because most of the participants were too busy stuffing their faces. Jake looked around and realized that the men, as usual, had separated from the women and staked out the dining and sunrooms as their own. They kept a wary eye on the proceedings in the parlor as Rose began to open wedding presents. Poor Evan was stuck beside her for the duration.

Jake finished his meal. He went to peek in on Lia and saw she was in an animated conversation with a slim redheaded girl in a wheelchair. The redhead intercepted his glance. Her eyes widened and she pointed him out to Lia. He beat a hasty retreat to the backyard.

Sam and Danny were nowhere in sight, but a man who looked as discomfited as Jake had set up an outpost at the edge of the garden where the lilac bushes grew thick and tall. "Jake Robbin," he said, breaking out into a grin. "Good to see you, man."

Jake walked over. The guy was tall, broad, shaggy-haired. "I'm sorry. Do I know you?"

"Noah Saari. I was a couple of years behind you in school."

"Yeah, yeah. I think I remember. You played basketball?"

"Some." They shook. "What about you?"

"Nah. Not enough to speak of." Basketball was the major sport in the local school, and Jake had been a star for a short time, until he'd been suspended from the team for carousing and breaking curfew. The coach had wanted Jake to come back, but he'd been such a hothead he had chosen to quit rather than knuckle under to the team rules. One misstep of many from his wild adolescence.

"I heard you were back in town," Noah said. "It's

been a long time. But I bet the old hometown hasn't changed."

"Trees are taller. Folks are older. That's about it."

"New crop of babies." Noah smiled. "Claire and I have one on the way."

"Congratulations," Jake said. "When's the kid due?"

"Another three months or so. Claire's hoping for a big baby, full term. She's mad at me because we were hitched only six months ago and if the baby comes early, people will think we had to rush the wedding."

Jake nodded. In Alouette, counting the months between wedding and delivery was still a popular pastime. He remembered his mother and her friend Alice whispering with relish about who was "PG," yet she'd shrieked like a banshee when the same had happened to her own daughter.

Noah rubbed his jaw. "You married?"

"Nope."

"You came in with someone, didn't you? The pretty blonde? I thought there was a daughter, too. She took off from here a little while ago with Danny Swanson."

"No, that's just a—you know. Her name's Lia Howard. She's staying in one of our cottages. My sister's friend."

"Oh, yeah. I remember when Beth Trudell was telling my wife about Tess hiring Lia at the library. But she had a different last name."

"Hmm. Well, she's divorced."

"That must be it."

They fell silent. "The women keep this stuff straight," Noah said after a minute, "but darn if I can."

Jake made a sound of agreement. "What was the name you heard?"

Noah shrugged. "You got me. Started with a P, maybe."

Jake remembered Lia stumbling over her last name when she'd first introduced herself. Understandable if she'd changed it after the divorce. But hadn't she been divorced for several years? And it seemed unusual that the kids also went by Howard.

Another piece of the puzzle.

Jake roused himself. "Which way did Danny go with Lia's daughter?"

"Out to the cliff."

The men parted with another handshake and a "See you around." Jake found the trail to the cliffs and emerged into the wild blue open after ducking past a few pine boughs. The rocks were streaked in shades of rose, cream and gray, set in jagged contours washed by the strong surf off the big lake.

Sam and Danny had climbed partway down the cliff-side to a flat rock with a spectacular vantage point. Their heads were together. Between their conversation and the sound of the waves, they didn't notice Jake's approach.

"He won't let me," Sam said. "He thinks he's a badass."

Jake kicked a stone off the side of the cliff. "I *know* I'm a badass."

The teenagers looked up guiltily. Sam flushed. "Can't you leave me alone?"

"I tried that. Ticked off your mother when she found out about it."

Sam rolled her eyes at Danny. He brushed his hair off his forehead and squinted up at Jake. "We were wondering if it would be all right if I drove Sam home. I got my license a month ago. My dad gave me his car for the day. We thought maybe we could stop for ice cream on the way."

Jake contemplated. "I don't know if it's a good idea to leave the party early."

"Rose won't care." Danny had a quick smile that flashed on and off like a firefly at night, same as Rose. "She told me that she'd leave early if she dared."

"Then it's okay by me." Jake nodded toward the house. "But you have to ask your mother, Sam. What she says goes."

"Really? It's okay?" Sam's face brightened considerably despite the raccoon eyes as she clambered up the rocks. "Thanks, Jake. I'll go see what she says."

Jake put a hand on Danny's arm as the boy followed. "She's just fourteen."

"I'll be fifteen by the end of the summer," Sam hollered. "I'm going into ninth grade. Sheesh."

Jake stared at Danny. "No funny business."

"Yeah, sure." Danny lowered his chin, and the crop of hair fell back into his eyes. "We'll be good."

And I'll be bad, Jake thought with smug satisfaction, watching them go. It was a win-win. Sam could be thrilled about ditching the grown-ups, and Jake would get what he wanted—a chance to be alone with Lia.

CHAPTER ELEVEN

"Stop fretting," Jake said. "Danny'll have her home before we get there. He's a fairly reliable kid. And besides, I spoke to him. I was a badass."

Lia wrinkled her nose. "You're not half the badass you pretend to be."

He leaned his arm against the open window, steering with one hand as the pickup coasted down Bayside Hill. "Don't tell anyone. I have a reputation to maintain."

"Do you mean the rep from being a big, bad Army Ranger?"

"And as one of the reckless Robbin boys."

"I heard someone call you Black Jack Junior. Are you named after your father?"

"Yep. But I've always been called Jake. My full name is Jackson Barrett Robbin." He glanced over at Lia. Too casually. "What's yours?"

Shivers raced across her skin. She rubbed her arms, not certain if she was responding to his question or to his proximity. "What does it matter?"

"Just getting to know you."

She swallowed. "Lia Kathleen Howard. I was born thirty-two and a half years ago in lower Michigan. My father was an insurance salesman who called himself an estate planner, and my mother was a housewife who thought she was Martha Stewart. They still have their same delusions of grandeur. I was their only child and ultimately a great disappointment. My tastes are simple. I like to play board games with the kids, do needlepoint and watch movies. My favorite meal is chicken cacciatore with chocolate cake for dessert. My goals are to own a house of my own and get my kids into college." She spread her hands. "There you have it. Me in a nutshell."

Jake went silent, but she could see him thinking when he finally said, "Then Howard's not your married name?"

"No. I went back to it."

"The children, too?"

"I don't remember saying that." She tucked her hands between her knees as they drove by the Berry Dairy. Why was he suspicious now? Or had he always been?

She breathed a sigh of relief when he dropped the subject. "Should we stop for ice cream? We can take it down to the marina and watch the sunset."

"No, thank you." Lia tried not to stare too openly as they passed. A group of teens was gathered in the parking lot, smoking and playing loud music. "Sam will accuse of us checking up on her."

"All right. No ice cream. Would you like to see the lighthouse?"

"Is that a metaphor?"

"That depends on if I light up your life."

Lia put her elbow up on the car door and pressed her knuckles against her smile. "You might."

Her answer had surprised him. He said nothing while he drove through town. Only when they turned onto a narrow dirt lane did he speak, in a thickened voice. "I think it's time we went to the lighthouse."

She looked out the window, catching glimpses of the lake through the trees on either side of the road. "Why do I feel as if I'm missing something here?"

Jake grinned. "'Going to the lighthouse' is sort of a tradition with new couples around here. You can probably guess why."

"Um, does this mean you're planning on doing something that I'd kill Sam for even thinking about?" She wasn't going to touch the "new couples" reference.

The pickup traveled through a shallow gully and up an incline. Suddenly the trees gave way and they were on the grounds of the lighthouse, which loomed above them, perched atop the highest point of a rocky peninsula with a panoramic view of the lake.

Jake shut off the engine. "We're here to watch the sunset. Anything else that happens is pure bonus."

Lia rubbed her sweaty palms on her lap. Her halter-top sundress was inexpensive cotton but colorful and pretty, with a flirty flared skirt. It wasn't made for the winds that picked up speed as they swept across miles of water. "Can we stay in the truck? I'm wearing high-heeled sandals and no sweater."

"Whatever you want." He reached in the storage space behind the seats and pulled out a creased denim jacket. "Wear this." He leaned over and slipped the garment around her shoulders.

"Thanks." She slid her hands through the sleeves. The jacket was heavy and smelled slightly of oil and leather. Inhaling, she pulled the collar up around her jaw. "So this is the popular make-out spot, huh?"

"It was when I was young and horny. But we also hung out on the rocks as a group and drank beer. The lighthouse was abandoned then."

"You know that Tess and her husband Connor own it now, right? He travels when he's researching a new book, so they only come out here for weekends and holidays pretty much. I guess. I mean, that's what she told me." She always chattered like a squirrel when she got nervous.

Jake stretched his arms out behind her on the seat and touched her right shoulder. "Don't be nervous."

She giggled girlishly. "This is weird. I haven't made out since I was a teenager."

"I doubt they're doing it any differently today."

"That's not what I hear."

"Yeah, maybe you're right. They're doing it a lot sooner and more often."

"I worry about Sam." Lia sighed. "And I really hope

she and Danny didn't see us driving out this way. I'd never hear the end of it."

"Big difference. You're legal."

She moved her shoulders, wanting him to touch her again. The decision that there could be no lasting relationship didn't have to stop her from enjoying their chemistry for a couple of minutes. Maybe longer. Her sex drive, dozing for years, had wakened. Nerve sensors were sparking and demanding appeasement. She was curious to discover how deep the attraction went.

A quick glance at Jake made her lips stick together. He was sprawled like a lazy lion surveying his kingdom. Large, male and potentially rapacious.

"Um, so…did you bring a lot of girls here in your day?"

"Not so many. Only the ones who liked to walk on the wild side."

Despite the disclaimer, Lia imagined that there'd been plenty of those. She'd never had such inclinations. Her parents had approved of Larry. He'd been on the basketball and volleyball teams, an honor student, the kind of boy who was always polite to adults. They never knew about the snide comments made behind their backs.

She'd been too naive to listen to the doubts at the back of her mind. The unexpected pregnancy had been so overwhelming she'd done exactly what Larry and her parents planned—the hasty wedding with a justice of the peace, the refusal of a college scholarship so she could work to help keep Larry in school, moving in with his folks.

"You're frowning," Jake said.

"Sorry."

"You don't have to apologize. Ever."

"I've been apologizing for the past fifteen years." First to her parents, then to Larry.

"That's over."

She gave him skeptical look. "Because you say so?"

"I can make it happen. But I'd like to hear you say so."

She sat tall. Lifted her chin. "It's over." Larry's psychological imprisonment, her unforgiving parents, the mistakes she'd made, the choices she hadn't. "All of it. That life is over. And I'm not sorry."

Jake's arms encircled her. He purred like a big cat, rumbly in his chest. "Mmm. That's my girl."

"I'm not—" His mouth covered hers, cutting off the protest. She closed her eyes, sank into the warmth of the kiss. Maybe she could be his girl for a while.

Pleasure slipped through her. Waves on the shore, softening her like loose sand. Jake's mouth was the undertow. Inexorable. Pulling her deep. He held her snug against his body as he leaned back against the length of the seat, keeping her on top. His hands were on her bottom, then in her hair, then spanning her waist. But always there was his mouth.

Kiss after kiss after kiss.

She quit thinking, worrying, deciding. Her body became liquid. She held his shoulders, scraped her cheek against his jaw, drank in his aroma. Slow and luxurious.

Kiss after kiss after kiss.

Jake was a surprise. There was no hurry or aggression. No demands or directions. He was easy. He kissed her as if he valued her. And when the pleasure turned into passion that burned too hot, that made her want to do the things she'd forbidden, it was finally he who stopped with a deep moan and obvious reluctance, clasping her hands tight against his chest.

She lifted her head, not really cognizant yet except to know that the sky was dark beyond their misty windows and the blood in her veins ran like quicksilver. "We missed the sunset."

BY MIDWEEK THE VOLATILE physical sensations had settled and Lia sank back into the normal routine. She had no idea what Jake was thinking about their trip to "the lighthouse." Other than a few discreet touches when he'd caress the small of her back or let his fingers linger after brushing away a mosquito, he gave no overt sign that their relationship had altered.

That was what you wanted, Lia scolded herself whenever she was feeling frustrated. No pressure. No expectations. A sexy interlude that came and went.

True, her libido was revved. But she could control it. She wasn't a love-struck teenager and neither was Jake. She had a life to pull together.

Lia was quickly given plenty of work at the library from Tess, who was taking time off because her husband was home for the summer. Lia gladly took on the extra hours. She planned a stringent budget and stuck to it other than a few small indulgences for the kids.

In return for the extra babysitting duties, she granted Sam more freedom. Jake washed and greased an old bike of Rose's and Sam used that to ride into town. She met Danny and his friends at the beach. She got to know a couple of girls her age and one day conceded to Lia that enrolling at Alouette High School in September might not be quite as bad as she'd thought.

The children's first missed visitation with Larry came and went. Lia worried at night, imagining how enraged he must be to have his control stolen. She wondered if he'd gone to the police even though he despised their authority. More likely he'd set a private investigator on her trail. She knew she'd done wrong and would soon have to face up to the consequences, but she hoped to regain her inner strength before the hatchet fell. When the time came, she would have to face Larry down at last.

"OF COURSE THERE WERE gang members," Sam said to the group of Danny's friends, exaggerating about her old neighborhood. "Lots of them."

"Girls, too?" asked Dara Niemi.

She was impressed by Sam—the piercing, the

styling, the 'tude. But she was only going into eighth grade. Kid stuff. Sam wanted the older kids to recognize her cool.

"Some girls." She tossed her head. "I might join when I go back."

"Why?" Danny asked. He was sitting on the hood of a car, with his feet up on the bumper, bouncing a basketball between his knees. The car was parked a short distance from the rusted-out rim of the public basketball court. The guys had been leaping off the hood to slam-dunk.

"Well…"

"The drugs, man," said one of the boys with a loud laugh. He knocked knuckles with Sam.

Her gaze slid to Danny. He was pretty much a straight arrow, although he'd tried the cigarettes some of the kids were passing around. So had Sam. A couple of puffs. She'd told them she'd had to cut back until she got the chance to lift a few packs to replenish her supply. The lies had just rolled off her tongue.

Jeremy started dancing goofy steps to the rap music blaring from the car radio. He flashed gang signs and some of the kids cheered.

Sam just shrugged. "That's not even right."

"Why don't you show us, city girl?" someone challenged.

She did a few quick moves she'd seen in a music video, then turned and sauntered away as if she was bored with the whole thing. She cocked a hip against the hot metal of the car and flicked her chin at Danny. "Not bad, huh?"

He spun the basketball between his palms. A shrug. "Yeah, sure."

Sam was disappointed. She turned her back on him and tuned into the conversation the others were having, about spray painting graffiti on some rocks along 525. Jeremy lamented the end of the tradition they'd had of painting their class year at the lighthouse point, Gull Rock, now that the property was privately owned.

"I'd do it anyway," Sam boasted.

Dara's mouth dropped open. "For real?"

"Anytime, anywhere."

LIA HAD AGREED TO WORK the second shift at the ice cream stand, from three to nine o'clock. She whipped up shakes, concocted banana-split sundaes and scooped ice cream until her arm hurt. At nine, she closed the window, took out the mop and sponges and scrubbed the place from top to bottom. By the time she locked up she was hot, sticky and achy.

The lake beckoned, cold and blue. She stared at it for a long while. If she'd had no reason to get home, she would have run down to the beach and jumped in the water like a carefree teenager.

A honking horn interrupted the thought. Jake's pickup roared into the parking lot and braked within inches of Lia. Her insides twisted when she saw the grim expression on his face. Howie and Kristen were with him, goggle-eyed.

"Lia, the police called. It's Sam."

The world spun away beneath her feet. She almost missed Jake's next words.

"She's in custody."

Lia lurched and grabbed onto the door of the pickup. "But she's all right? It wasn't an accident?"

"No. No. I didn't mean to—" He stopped, backtracked. "She was picked up for vandalism."

A different sort of jolt rocked Lia. "What?"

"I don't know the details. They called from the police station ten minutes ago. I didn't want to wait for you to get home from work." He scowled. "Even though waiting a while in custody might do Sam some good."

Lia bristled. "I want her out of there. Now."

"Don't get crazy. She's not being mistreated."

"Jake! She's my daughter." Lia looked at the tears welling in Kristen's eyes and made an effort to scale back her emotion. "Don't cry, Krissy. Everything's going to be okay."

The little girl sniffled. "Sam's in prison?"

"'Course not, stupid." Howie pushed his glasses up his nose. "They don't put juvenile delinquents in prison."

"Mommy, is Sam a ju—a juve—"

"No, she's not." Lia avoided Jake's scowl. She lowered her voice to address him. "Can you bring these two home while I go and get Sam?"

·"Are you sure you don't want me with you?" He attempted a leavening grin. "I have experience in these matters."

She shook her head. "I hope I don't need a lawyer."

"I doubt it. Corky—Deputy Corcoran—said you just have to come in to discuss the matter when you pick her up. He wouldn't tell me what she'd done."

"I have to go." Lia started off, then turned back. "Where is the police station?"

Jake gave her directions to the lower level of the old brick courthouse on a downtown corner. Not until she was in her car and driving the short distance did Lia start thinking about presenting herself to the police. What if there'd been a bulletin sent out to all law enforcement agencies—a kind of top ten Most Wanted of child snatching and custody fights?

Walking down the steps into the station was her own version of descending into hell. Only for one of her children could she have done it. Irony at its best, since that was also why she'd gotten into trouble with the law in the first place.

Lia gave her name at the front desk, speaking barely above a whisper. Deputy Corcoran seemed to recognize her, but he made no comment about their first meeting. He escorted her to an office, letting her know that Sheriff Bob had come in special for this conference.

The small room was filled with people, some sitting, several standing against the wall—concerned parents and a group of teenagers exchanging guilty glances.

The sheriff was holding court from behind his desk, but he bobbed up at Lia's arrival. "Sheriff Bob," he said cheerfully. "Good to meetcha."

She shook his hand. Her tongue moved thickly with her name. "Lia Howard."

"Who?" He reached for paperwork.

"My daughter's here," Lia said quickly. "Saman-tha…?" She twisted, looking for Sam.

"Ah, yes. You're our final guest. Have a seat."

One empty chair remained, squeezed into the corner beside Sam, who was trying to look defiant except that she wouldn't meet her mother's eyes. She'd done something strange with her hair, added mousse or grease so it stood up in a ridge down the center of her skull. With the dark eye makeup, a black tank, jeans shorts and her studded leather jewelry, she did look like a juvenile delinquent.

Even though Lia knew that trouble came in many disguises, she was embarrassed that she'd let Sam get so punk. She also saw how the others in the room reacted to her daughter's getup. At least their kids, the parents seemed to say with every surreptitious glance, looked "normal."

Sheriff Bob cleared his throat. "All righty then. As you may or may not know, we're here to discuss an instance of vandalism out at the lighthouse. Corky caught these kids spray painting the rocks. They're all to blame—we're playing no favorites here. But we do seem to have a ringleader."

Lia's face got hot. The sheriff was staring directly at Sam.

"What do you have to say for yourself, young lady?"

"IT WASN'T ONLY ME." Sam shot out of the car and slammed the door. She ran down the path. "Why do I get all the blame?"

"You were the only one caught red-handed," Lia yelled an instant before the cottage door also slammed.

"I hate you!" Sam screeched from inside the house.

Lia muttered a curse word under her breath. She had a vicious headache.

"You're not going to let her get away with that kind of disrespect, are you?" Jake said. He sat on the doorstep of the main house, watching. Judging.

Lia had enough misery on her plate without him heaping on another helping. Tiredly she paused beside the car and rubbed her forehead. "What do you expect me to do?"

"Lay down the law."

Her head snapped up. "You're a fine one to speak. I left her at home with Howie and Kristen. You told Sam it was all right to go and meet her friends. She shouldn't have been out so late in the first place."

"Did she say I also told her to be back by eight?"

Lia slumped. "No, she didn't mention that. I'm sorry. You're not to blame. I'm just at my wit's end."

"I thought it would be okay," Jake added in a

quieter voice. "You said that you wanted her to have more freedom."

"Obviously she can't handle it." Lia walked toward him, dragging her feet.

Howie's silhouette showed in one of the lighted windows of Jake's house. He was watching them with his chin on the sill. The poor kid. With all the upheaval, he wouldn't be able to sleep tonight.

"What did she do?" Jake asked.

"There was a group of them. They were spray painting graffiti on the rocks by the lighthouse." Lia had mixed emotions about the incident, including an odd sense of guilt that seemed to spring from her recent trip to the same place. "The sheriff called Sam the ringleader."

Jake's eyes were very dark and reflective in the low light. She wondered if he was also remembering their kisses. "How much trouble is she in?" he asked.

"No official record. The sheriff seemed as interested in keeping the parents happy as he was in meting out punishment. Sam has to write a letter of apology to Connor and Tess Reed and go with the other kids to clean up their mess."

"Was Danny involved?"

"Apparently not. He was there when they came up with the plan, but Sam said he told her not to go. I don't know why she did. I couldn't get much out of her except tantrum and tears."

Jake shrugged. "Teenage rebellion doesn't always have a reason."

"Yeah, but I can guess why she's acting out."

Lia closed her eyes, waiting for Jake to jump on that, but he kept quiet. The buzz of insects and shrill *cheep* of peepers filled the silence. The pounding in her head lessened by a few degrees. The sheriff had made no sign of recognition at her name, nor held her back for separate questioning.

"Don't blame yourself, Lia."

"I don't. I blame her father." Not entirely true. Lia had many regrets over the way she'd handled things, starting with being too permissive with Sam.

"What did he do? Did he ever hurt you? Or the kids?"

"Only if you count mental abuse."

"Of course I do. My mother lived in terror of my father's moods. Even when he wasn't drinking, he could be cruel."

Lia pinned her gaze on Jake. "And you?"

"I was born with a thick skin."

"And Rose?"

"She grew one. Mostly she stayed out of the way." Jake stood and followed her as she moved away from the house so Howie wouldn't overhear. He stood near her with his hands in his pockets. "We were talking about what happened to you."

She blew out a breath, trying to decide how much to say. "Larry wasn't the man I thought I married. It's hard to remember that I loved him once, but I did. We had some good years. There were little signs of his obsessive personality in how he wanted to control me even at the start, but they were easy to overlook. I wanted to please him. Gradually, though, the criticism got worse."

She continued walking, leaving her cottage behind, which was silent and dark, and moving along the path to the next. Her irritation with Jake had eased. Even Sam's bad behavior was understandable. Except she didn't know how to correct it.

"I think sometimes that Sam must be dealing with the same kind of mixed-up feelings that I keep inside." Lia ran her fingers over the branch of a pine. "Larry killed my self-esteem. He bitched about everything. How I kept the house, how I cooked. The kids. My clothes, my looks, my lack of enthusiasm for—um, in the bedroom." She hurried past that slip. "Even after the divorce, he wouldn't let go. He'd show up at my jobs, he'd call and hang up. And even after I got a court order to keep him away, he'd try to spy on me through the kids."

She stopped. That was enough.

Jake stood beside her, his arms folded across his chest. "So that's why you moved up here—to get away from Larry?"

"Sort of."

"Will he follow?"

"He might." She stared at Jake's forearms, trying to decipher the tattoos in the deepening dusk. Intricate designs of military insignia, an eagle with spread wings, a wolf, a thorny vine that coiled above one wrist. The letters RLTW were prominent on his right arm. She hoped they weren't the initials of a past love.

"Lia." He reached to touch her, then stopped with his fingertips under her chin. "Talk to me."

She blinked. "What do you want to know?"

"Are you afraid of your ex-husband?"

"Afraid?" She turned her head aside. "I don't know if *afraid* is the word…" Afraid that he'd hurt her physically? No. Afraid that he'd take her children away? Yes. A million times yes.

Jake cleared his throat. "There's something I've been thinking about, and maybe now is the time for me to speak."

Lia backed away a step. She gave a fluttery laugh. "Oh, I don't know about that. I've had enough drama for today."

"I'm not planning to add to it. In fact, I think I'll be taking care of all your problems at once."

She blinked. Oh, dear. "That's a big order."

He stood among the towering trees, which couldn't dwarf him. A tall man. A hard man. An honest man.

Although Lia couldn't say how she knew, she sensed what was coming. Nevertheless, she nearly keeled over into a faint when Jake said with complete gravity, "I want to marry you."

CHAPTER TWELVE

"MARRY ME?" LIA PUT out her hands for balance. Her eyes grew bigger and bigger. "Marry me?" She burst into a hearty chuckle. Forced. "You've known me for less than two weeks. Why would you want to marry me?"

Jake hadn't known what to expect, but he'd never imagined laughter. He clenched his hands and tried to remember all the practical reasons he'd been lining up in his mind for the past week.

But they'd flown the coop. All he could think of was the way her mouth tasted. The scent of her hair. Cupping her rear end in his hands.

"Here's another question," she said. "Why would I want to marry you?"

"It's for your benefit," he blurted.

"Yeah?" She ran shaky fingers through her hair. "Maybe you're right, but that makes me feel great. Real great." She turned and marched away, flinging her head like Sam.

"Wait. Let me explain."

She whirled on him and poked a finger into his

chest. "I don't need to listen to an explanation about how my life is a complete mess and you're sacrificing yourself for the cause. Do you really think I'd jump all over the offer because it's to my benefit? Do you really think that I'm desperate enough to want another husband who'll constantly tell me what to do and where to go?" She stabbed the finger. "You know where you can go with your charity proposal, Jake Robbin? Straight to hell."

She stormed off again.

"Lia," he called. "Be reasonable."

Her answer carried through the trees. "No thanks! You have no right to tell me how to act. If I want to be unreasonable, I'll be goddamn unreasonable."

"That's your problem, you know." He moved fast to catch up before she disappeared inside the cottage. "You're looking at this in an emotional way."

She stared with the whites of her eyes showing. "Marriage proposals are emotional. Usually."

"In this case…" He lost track of his words again. Her glare packed quite a punch. There suddenly seemed to be so many holes in his ready-made-family theory that he could see daylight on the other side.

"Yes? What about this—" she gestured at herself "—so-called case?"

"I'm trying to say that if you'll carefully consider the practical reasons, you'll understand why a marriage between us makes sense."

Some of the heat ebbed out of Lia's eyes. She

sighed. "Jake, I know you mean well. And I know what you're going to say. You can give the kids and me a home and security. Protection from Larry. I get it. I can—" She made a strangled sound. "I can even appreciate it. You win the medal for good conduct, honorable intentions, all that stuff, okay?"

She folded her arms and tucked her hands under her elbows. "But what I don't get is what you think *you'd* get out of a marriage of convenience."

He drew back his head. "Who said I wanted a marriage of convenience?"

She threw up her hands. "Okay, now I'm puzzled. Isn't that what you're offering?"

"No. I want—" His heart gave an extrahard thump. "I want a real marriage."

"Uhhh…" Lia was finally at a loss for words. She stared at him without blinking, then finally said, barely above a whisper, "What does that mean?"

"There are all kinds of marriages, but generally it means making a lasting commitment. Caring, family, sex. You know the drill. Joining lives."

"Sex," she said faintly. "You want sex."

"Yes. But that's not all."

"There are easier ways to get sex than marrying me."

"Will you stop? I said that it's not all about sex."

"Uh-huh. I notice you didn't mention love."

Jake had figured she'd latch on to that point. Most women did. He was willing to make a concession. "Eventually we might learn to love each other."

"After we're married?"

"It happens."

"Kind of backward though."

"Seems sensible to me. Since so many couples start out in love, then get married and eventually fall out of love, why can't we switch the order around?"

"But what if we don't learn to love each other?" she asked with a heavy—and clearly skeptical—emphasis.

"We'd still have the other benefits of marriage."

"Pardon me, Jake, but I still don't understand why you're so gung ho. You don't even seem like the marrying type. Rose said as much. And other than sex, you haven't said what you expect to get out of the deal."

"I'd get a family."

She was taken aback. "You want a family?"

"Yeah, I do. I never saw the reason for a family when I was in the military and being sent off on dangerous assignments at a moment's notice. I saw how many couples broke up or came to a tragic end. After I was discharged, I drifted for a while, trying to figure out what I wanted to do with the rest of my life. For the first time, I realized I might get lonely living alone. And now I'm here. I'm ready to settle down."

"Just like that." Lia's voice had gone flat again, just when he'd thought he was getting somewhere. "So the upshot is that you'd get an instant family, a regular sex life and someone to cook and clean. In return you perform your husbandly duties. Which I'm certain you'd do very well. No doubt about that."

"Exactly. It would be a mutually beneficial arrangement."

"Cut-and-dried. Like a business deal."

He was ready for her to launch into the romance thing again and geared up to defend himself. It wasn't that he couldn't imagine loving Lia. That was, in fact, surprisingly easy to do. His problem was in believing that the love would last forever, the way it was supposed to but rarely did.

Nope. Even if the love issue was a deal breaker, he refused to make promises that he might not be able to keep. He'd tried that once and learned it took two to make a marriage.

Lia didn't go there. She looked at him with cool eyes. A small smile hovered near her lips but never quite landed. "I see now that you've thought it all through. Very commendable. Except that you forgot one thing."

She angled toward him, lowering her voice to a harsh whisper. "You don't know me. You don't know who I really am or what I'm capable of. You have no idea what kind of trouble you'd be getting into by marrying me."

He had dropped his head forward to listen. Her words shocked him into pulling back. What had she done—poisoned Larry with arsenic and buried him in the backyard?

Lia straightened. "I can be honorable, too, Jake. And that's why I'm refusing your…deal. But thank you very much for the offer." With a brittle dignity, she stepped up to her door and turned the knob. "Good night."

LONG PAST MIDNIGHT, Lia was awake, replaying Jake's proposal—if you could call it that—in her mind. Many words had poured out of her mouth in response, but in the quiet dark she'd come to realize that her refusal had a flaw.

The flaw was that she'd fallen in love with him.

There was irony, as well, because she loved him for the same traits that had led to his idea of making a marriage partnership with her. That he would even dream up the offer, let alone voice it, showed his character. He was honorable, dependable, generous, kind. Not to mention smoking-hot.

He also tended to be bossy and single-minded. Warning flags for her.

Then there was the unavoidable truth that marrying Jake would be good for her and the kids in many ways. She wondered how much of that was mixed up in her growing feelings for him. While she didn't particularly want to be practical, she wasn't a starry-eyed bride, either. Marriage wasn't about valentines and roses. Even those that began with falling in love.

He'd actually made a lot of sense.

She was the one messing up the plan.

Lia leaned her head against the hard, curved branches of the twig armchair. She was huddled, wrapped in a robe. In the bedroom, the kids slept blissfully unaware. Even Sam, who'd expected a lecture that Lia had been too wrung-out to deliver. She couldn't have put any spirit into it after working up all that outrage for her big kiss-off speech to Jake.

She moaned at the memory. The only problem with making an exit in real life was that it was real life. In other words, messy. She'd had to knock on his door five minutes later to collect Howie and Kristen.

Jake's hollow look had rocked her. Was it possible he'd invested more feeling into his oh-so-reasonable marriage plan than he'd admitted to?

Lia had no answers. She knew only that she was more complication than Jake had bargained for and that she deserved a man who didn't have to learn to love her.

Refusing him had been the right thing to do. At least she hoped so.

Maybe she could convince herself and finally get some sleep.

But only if that damn owl would stop hooting!

JAKE WAS WASHING HIS lunch dishes and thinking what a pitiful lot they were—one plate, one knife, one glass—when he heard a car arriving outside, followed by the short burst of a siren. The engine stopped, doors creaked, footsteps fell. He hurried to the front door, drying his hands on his jeans.

Lia had come outside. Sam hovered in the doorway behind her, looking ghostly as she stared at the visitors.

A cop car. Both Sheriff Bob and Deputy Corcoran had emerged.

For Sam? With a siren? That didn't make a whole lot of sense to Jake. He charged out of the house and blocked the officers' path, acknowledging them with a nod. "Sheriff. Corky. What brings you out this way?"

Sheriff Bob chuckled. "Just like old times, eh, Jake?"

He didn't smile. "Very old times." He glanced over his shoulder at Lia's stricken face. He wanted to tell her not to be so scared, but he settled on deflection. "So you're here to arrest me, huh?"

The joke fell flat, especially when Corky spoke up. "Not you, Jake."

Sheriff Bob aimed a quelling look at his deputy. "I'm afraid a serious issue has come up." He tilted to one side to see past Jake. "Ma'am? Are you Lia Kathleen Howard Pogue?"

There was a long silence before Lia answered in a thin voice. "Yes."

Sheriff Bob unfolded a paper. "Of Cadillac, Michigan? Mother of Samantha, Howard and Kristen Pogue, ages fourteen, ten and four?"

Jake turned. The blood had drained from Lia's face. She said, "Yes," a second time and buckled slightly at the knees. He grabbed hold of her, and for a moment she leaned into his chest before deliberately pushing him away.

She straightened her shoulders. "Yes, that's me."

Sam collapsed bonelessly to the doorstep and began to cry. Howie and Kristen watched from the other side of the screen door, their faces and hands pressed to the mesh.

"The kids, Jake," Lia said. Her eyes were electric. "Will you take the kids?"

He nodded even though he had no idea what was going on. "What's this about?" he demanded of Sheriff Bob and was alarmed by how much his belligerent voice echoed his father's.

"Settle down, boy." The sheriff watched Jake warily. He hitched up his belt. "It's a custody matter."

"I see."

Lia walked over to Sam. She knelt to comfort her sobbing daughter, speaking in a low voice. Howie and Kristen spilled out of the house and clung to their mom, looking confused and frightened.

Impotence infused Jake. There seemed nothing he could do to ease their fear and pain. It was private. He wasn't a part of the family. Yet.

Sheriff Bob approached with the deputy on his heels. "I'm sorry, Mrs. Pogue, but I'll have to ask you to come with me."

Lia looked up. Her face was tearstained. "Are you arresting me?"

"Sorry, ma'am, but I've got to. There's a court order. The children missed a visitation with their father, a Mr. Lawrence Pogue of Cadillac, Michigan. He's filed a complaint in family court there."

"We didn't want to go," Sam said with a fierce intensity. "You can't make us."

"That's not up to me, young lady." The sheriff nodded at the deputy.

Corky stepped forward and took hold of Lia's elbow, urging her to her feet. He was reaching for his handcuffs when he caught Jake's eye. Jake shook his head. Corky flushed and let his hand drop. "I'll escort you to the car, ma'am."

Lia wiped her face and tucked her hair behind her ears. "What happens to my children?"

"I'm sorry," the sheriff said, "but they'll have to go with a court-appointed guardian and then to foster care until the matter is settled."

"Oh, God. Please don't do that. Can't Jake take them until I'm released?"

Sheriff Bob hesitated. "Officially, no."

Jake put his hand on the man's shoulder. "Do me a favor, Bob. You know I'm not going anywhere. I'll post bail for Lia, vouch for her, whatever I have to do to get her out fast. There's no sense in sending the children away."

"She could run off with them again."

"I won't let that happen."

The sheriff hemmed and hawed, but in the end he agreed to leave the kids with Jake. Meanwhile, Corky had put Lia into the back of the squad car.

The officers climbed into the front. Jake went and spoke to Lia through the window. She looked small and vulnerable but was holding on to her dignity like a pit bull.

"I should have told you," she said. "I thought—I thought it would be better if you weren't involved. But now…"

He was involved. And he wouldn't fail her. "Don't worry. I'll take care of everything."

She bowed her head. "I'm such a hypocrite."

"You're not," he said.

She looked at him with sorrowful eyes and mouthed, "I'm sorry."

The sheriff started the car.

Jake tore himself away. "Rose will come to look after the kids. I'll be ten minutes behind you. Just hold on." He watched until the squad car had swung onto Blackbear Road, then turned to face Lia's children.

Sam sat on the doorstep with Kristen hugging her from behind. Howie was wandering around in the grass, mumbling and biting his fingernails. Jake couldn't think what to say to them. He went to Howie first, put his arms around the boy's shoulders and gave him a quick hug.

He knelt near the girls and opened his arms. "C'mere, all of you."

Although Sam resisted for a moment with a sulky frown, Kristen threw herself into Jake's arms, linking all four of them in a loose embrace. "Why did the police take Mommy?"

"They only wanted to talk to her."

"It's Dad's fault." Howie rubbed at his running nose. His eyes were obscured behind misty glasses, but the tremor in his voice and the way he gulped were enough to pierce even Jake's heart. "He turned her in."

Jake cradled Kristen's head, not wanting her to hear. "We'll talk about it later." He stood and nudged the two youngest toward the door. "Go inside now. I'll be along in a minute."

Once they were gone, he was about to question Sam when she burst into a wail. "It's my fault—my fault Mom was arrested."

"Why do you—"

"Because the police asked my name and I forgot and I said Pogue. Mom told us we had to use Howard now in case they were looking for us, but I forgot. I was scared." She choked. "I should have told her and I didn't. If I told her, we coulda got away in time."

"Running would've only made things worse."

"Yeah, but what about Mom? What's gonna happen to her?"

"I don't know for sure, but it shouldn't be too bad."

Sam's lashes were pale brown without mascara. Her eyes were red, begging Jake for reassurance. "I don't want to go and live with my dad. I know I said I did, but it's not true."

"Your mom knows that."

Sam darted at Jake and threw her arms around his middle. She pressed her face against his chest. "Tell her I didn't mean to get her arrested and that I said I'll be good from now on."

He gave Sam's back an awkward pat, then softened

and rubbed a comforting circle between her bony shoulder blades. "You can tell her yourself. I'm bringing her home. I promise I'm bringing her home as soon as possible."

FIGURES TUMBLED AROUND and around in Lia's head. Money for the lawyer, money for bail, money for gas to travel out of town for the hearings, then more money for the lawyer, unless she got a court-appointed attorney. "What did you pay the lawyer, again?" she asked Jake while staring steadily out the window. She was in a daze.

"It doesn't matter."

"I have to pay you back."

"Forget about the money. That's not what's important."

"Easy to say when you have it."

He glanced over. Worried about her. She tried to summon the energy to show some animation, tell him how grateful she was or even to smile. She failed. Focusing on the money was easier than dealing with the bigger issues. She had no courage remaining to confront them.

"The lawyer thinks you'll be okay. It was only one missed visitation."

She closed her eyes. "So far, as long as I go back."

"She said we can negotiate a new agreement allowing you to live here."

"She doesn't know Larry."

"He'll make trouble?"

"Guaranteed."

The pickup slowed. Lia saw they were almost at the cottages and suddenly a panicky fear enveloped her. The numbness had been better. "Pull over. Please."

Jake complied. Blackbear was a two-lane country road, little traveled. After the engine stopped, there was only the sound of the forest and the wind. She tried to suck in a deep breath, but her chest was constricted. For a couple of weeks she'd tasted freedom. Now Larry had his hands locked around her neck again.

"What is it, Lia?"

She rubbed at her throat. "I don't— What will I say to the kids? They need to feel secure." Her voice gained strength. "I shouldn't have done this. Run away. But when Larry said he was taking me back to court to sue for full custody, I had no hope left. Every cent I'd saved had already gone for attorney's fees and he knew it. He was hoping I'd come crawling to him and beg for mercy."

"But running only made it worse."

"I hoped I wouldn't get caught." She undid the seat belt, not remembering when she'd fastened it or walked to the truck. "I guess I make a lousy criminal."

"Sam slipped up with the name."

"What?"

"The vandalism—she gave her real name. There must have been an APB out on you. She was kind of broken up about it after you left. Blaming herself."

Lia squeezed her eyes shut. "I expected too much of them. Kids can't be fugitives."

"I doubt they think of it that way. All they want is to be with you."

"Even Sam?"

"She had a couple of scares. She's waiting for you, ready to make up and be good."

Lia could almost smile. "For a while, maybe. Small blessings."

Jake stroked her hair. He leaned over and kissed her gently on the lips. "Don't worry so much. The kids don't want explanations right now. They just want you."

"OF COURSE SHE REFUSED you," Rose said with total exasperation as she took away Jake's dinner plate and set out fresh glasses of iced tea tinkling with ice cubes. "What did you expect?"

"I thought she'd see the sense behind it and be grateful."

"Grateful? Argh!" Rose reached across the table and grabbed him by the ear. She tugged it. He batted her away. "You're such an idiot. Such a man."

"Wait a minute," Evan put in. "Let's not malign an entire gender. I proposed properly, didn't I?"

"We were standing under a basketball hoop in the school gym and I had a hole in my sock." Although Rose's tone was sarcastic, she looked at her husband with soft eyes. "But I suppose it was romantic all the same." Her attention returned to Jake. "Him, though.

Forgetaboutit. No woman wants to be told all the practical reasons why she should marry."

"But—"

Rose overrode Jake. "No buts about it. Not even if there are practical reasons. Trust me on this, all right? Lia was probably worried that you'd ask her to sign a contract next. No wonder she called it a business deal."

Jake was disgruntled. He'd come to the Grants' house to give Lia privacy with her children for their reunion. Rose had fed him since he'd forgotten to eat during a day spent wrangling with lawyers and police and finally making bail. Somehow he'd ended up telling the entire story of his proposal and how Lia had reacted. He'd expected surprise, delight, maybe admiration for doing the upstanding thing by Lia and her family. Evan had nodded through parts of the tale, but Rose had turned gosh-darned female on Jake. His tomboy sister really had changed.

"So is it hopeless?" he said, his voice gone guttural. The screws tightened whenever he thought about Lia driving away in the squad car and the faces on her children as they'd watched. He'd been a madman, racing after her in his pickup. He'd stormed into the police station. They'd told him to wait. And wait some more. Fortunately he'd cooled down and realized that this was a case where a cooler head would prevail.

By the end of the day he was more determined

than ever. Why couldn't Lia—or Rose, for that matter—see reason?

He stared at his bulging knuckles. "You think there's any way I can persuade Lia to marry me?"

Rose's eyes narrowed. "Oh, she'll marry you."

Elation pumped into Jake. He deflated just as fast. "You mean she's desperate because of the arrest."

"Not only that."

He studied Rose's face, not sure if he should believe her. His kid sister was a wily one. No telling what she'd discussed with Lia. "Then what?"

"You really are an idiot, Jake. Here's the big secret. She has feelings for you."

"Uh, great. So what's the holdup?" Jake looked at Evan for help.

"You're on your own with that one, pal."

"Jake." Rose punched him in the biceps. "Lia wants to know that your proposal isn't completely pragmatic. She wants a little romance."

He scowled. "I don't do romance."

"Then you shouldn't be proposing. A marriage without romance is doomed to failure."

Jake weighed the advantages of confessing that he wasn't completely unemotional. He just wasn't good at talking out loud about it. Why did he have to when actions spoke louder than words?

He coughed. "There have been arranged marriages for centuries."

"These are modern times. Women have other expectations." Rose glanced at Evan. "Most men, too." Her eyes returned to Jake. "All you have to do is give an inch or two. I know it's in you. There's no way you'd have come up with this plan unless you had at least an inkling of genuine feeling for Lia. You may be a tough guy, but you're not heartless."

"I suppose I can try." Jake shifted around in his chair while he mulled the possibilities. "I have a problem with making promises that almost no one can keep. Undying love and all that junk."

"That's very cynical." Rose exchanged a smile with Evan. "I used to be almost that cynical."

"And true love changed all that?" Jake scraped his hair back from his face. "Never gonna happen."

"Is this because of that woman, what's-her-name—Cherise?"

"Who?" He suspected that the blank space inside him was showing on his face.

Rose backed off and switched to his present dilemma. "I can help if you want. Heaven knows I'm no expert, but between us we should be able to come up with the right words to propose."

He shook his head. "I'd better do this on my own."

"Fine. But don't screw it up again."

Evan had been patiently following the discussion. Finally he gave Rose a nudge. "You're not going to ask what's the rush?" He scratched his head. "Am I the only one here who thinks proposing marriage after two weeks is jumping the gun?"

Jake grunted. "Normally I'd agree, but I know what I'm doing."

"You're positive?"

"I'm positive."

Rose grinned as if she had a secret. "Maybe you should think about why you're so positive."

Jake felt heat rising up his throat. "Don't look at me that way. It's not such a strange idea. I'm ready to settle down, that's all. Like I told Lia, acquiring an entire family at once is far easier than going through all that diapering and teething nuisance."

Rose snickered. "Good grief. If that's what you said to Lia, you need even more help than I imagined."

CHAPTER THIRTEEN

"CANDLES," HOWIE SAID. "In the movies, they always have lots and lots of candles."

Kristen ran her stuffed animal over Jake's tattooed forearm. "I'll give you Cuddlebunny. Mommy likes when he kisses her. She says it tickles."

"Don't be stupid, Krissy. Mom doesn't want to kiss Cuddlebunny." Sam looked knowingly at Jake, hovering for an instant between disapproval and encouragement. His jaw gritted until she said, "Mom doesn't really like champagne that much. You should get her roses. And maybe a box of chocolates. She says chocolate makes her feel happy."

"Candles, flowers, chocolate," Jake said. "Check."

Kristen stared, bug-eyed as a hypnotist.

"Cuddlebunny," he added.

She beamed. "Check."

Howie fingered the side pieces of his glasses. "You could take her to a fancy restaurant."

"Maybe…"

"Maybe not," Sam said. "Mom likes privacy."

Jake was relieved, especially because he knew very

well he was risking another rejection. Lia had a stubborn streak, whether or not she was in a bind and plain common sense should tell her to accept. Except he wasn't supposed to be thinking sensibly anymore. He was supposed to think like a woman.

"And you have to go down on one knee when you propose," Howie said.

Jake balked. "That's hokey. Right, Sam?"

She fingered her hair. The blue tips had been trimmed away, making her an ordinary dishwater blonde. Jake would've paid her good money to take the stud out from beneath her lip, but he'd learned she was more apt to come to that decision if he kept his mouth shut.

"It is hokey," she said.

He let out a sigh of relief.

"But you should do it anyway." Was there a glint of payback in her eye? "Mom would think it was real romantic."

Jake was not going onto his knee to propose. To distract them, he waved at the yard. "How about I ask her here?"

They all looked. Even though the weeds were pulled, the grass shorn and several of the cottages freshened up, the area wasn't the most romantic spot. After a short silence, Sam spoke. "I guess we could fix it up."

"Like a party," Kristen said with a bounce. "Balloons and stuff."

Jake held up his hands. "Hold on. Let's not go overboard." He thought of the chocolates and roses and bunny rabbit. Too late. He was going to look like a fool whether or not he kneeled. If this didn't qualify as giving an inch—hell, at least a mile in his estimation—he didn't know what would.

THE NEXT EVENING Howie led a blindfolded Lia out of their cottage. She walked with her hands out, playing up her predicament by plaintively asking for someone to tell her what was going on. The only answer was Kristen's giggle.

Lia had come home from work and been swept inside by her daughters, who'd been silly with excitement as they'd told her to put on her best dress. While Kristen had danced around flapping her arms like a fairy, Sam had applied makeup and fixed Lia's hair, switching back and forth between a sophisticated upsweep and keeping it loose and wavy. She'd wanted her mother to wear heels, but Lia had insisted on a pair of beaded flip-flops. She'd worn pumps for five hours at the library and her feet were protesting.

They refused to explain their purpose. Lia enjoyed herself anyway. Sam had loved to play beauty shop as a little girl, with her mom as the customer. There were snapshots of Lia smeared with lipstick and blush, her hair in a half dozen ponytails with multicolored bows. She wondered if Sam remembered.

"Quit smiling, Mom. I have to do the gloss."

Kristen made fish lips. "I want some."

Eventually Howie had appeared at the door and announced, "We're ready."

We're ready, Lia was thinking as Howie tugged her forward. Obvious what that meant. Her nerves knew, too. They were jumping double Dutch in the hollow of her stomach.

"We're here," Howie proclaimed. He was jittery. His hand was clammy in Lia's.

"Can I take the blindfold off?"

She felt Sam behind her, undoing the knotted scarf. It was whisked away. Howie made a flourish like a magician. "Voilà!"

Lia blinked. The small yard beside the main house had been transformed. Strings of Christmas lights festooned the trees. The patio table had been spread with a tablecloth and topped with a group of flickering candles and real china and flatware. Clusters of balloons were tied to the chair backs with curly ribbon.

Jake stood at the center of it all, smiling rather sheepishly. He looked handsome but very different in a dress shirt with an open collar and neat trousers instead of jeans. He held a bouquet of red roses.

"You're having dinner with Jake," Howie said, pushing her forward.

"And Cuddlebunny," Kristen added, pointing to the plush rabbit who sat on one of the chairs.

Jake's expression grew even more sheepish.

"Jeez, you guys." Sam grabbed Kristen's hand and

Howie's arm and towed them toward Jake's house. "We'll be right back with the dinner."

"Dinner?" Lia inhaled a melange of home cooking, scented wax and the chemical tang of Raid.

Jake held out her chair. "I was cooking all afternoon with the kids. Between us, we knew just enough to mess up every pot, pan and bowl in the house. Don't count on this dinner being edible."

Lia sat. He thrust the roses at her. "For you."

"Thanks." She admired them, almost afraid to ask. "What's the occasion? My being sprung from jail?"

"Uh, no." Jake was unusually skittish, not meeting Lia's eyes. "We wanted to do something nice for you."

Sounds of thuds and clatter came from the kitchen. "You cooked. With the kids." Lia fingered the rose petals. "I'm stunned."

"We get up to a lot of mischief when you're not around."

"So it seems."

An awkward silence fell, punctuated by Sam's voice giving orders inside. "Did you hear anything new from the lawyer?" Jake asked.

Lia shook her head. "She's contacting Larry's attorney, going to try to get them to drop charges and negotiate a truce, but good luck with that. I've tried."

"You don't speak his language."

"Larry's?" She made a face. "Who does?"

"I might."

"Man to man, huh?" She'd hoped never to see Larry

again, but that was impossible. He'd always be in her life, like a bad dream that might appear at any time.

"Sometimes that's what it takes," Jake said.

She cocked her head. "Hands off my woman—that kind of thing?"

He paused. "Let's change the subject. We're supposed to be having a good time."

"It's not easy to get in the mood," she admitted. "At the library today, two different people asked me if I was really arrested. One heard that it was for kidnapping." She winced. "Ouch."

"That's rough. I'm sorry."

She tried to shrug it off. "I've been a nice girl all my life. Having a reputation as a jailbird takes some getting used to."

"People will understand once the real story gets out."

"Should they? I *am* guilty."

"Justifiably."

The back door of the house opened and they stopped the conversation. Sam, Howie and Kristen arrived bearing heavy dishes and a bottle of wine. Jake leaped up to help.

Lia was flabbergasted when Sam lifted the lid of a steaming casserole dish. The smell of tomato and garlic was enticing. "Chicken cacciatore! My favorite."

Kristen put down a basket of rolls, slightly burned on the bottom. "It's a roman'ic dinner, Mom."

"Very. I'm impressed." Lia gave the roses to Sam,

then took up a serving spoon. There was also a salad and green beans. She considered the two place settings. "What about you three?"

They answered at once. "We'll have ours inside."

"Jake wants to be alone with you."

"To get roman'ic."

The children retreated. Lia and Jake busied themselves with the meal. He didn't say much but chewed steadily.

She forked up the chicken and pasta. "You remembered."

He nodded, his brow creasing adorably. "Is it okay?"

"Delicious." Overcooked pasta, but she'd never say so. "Did you really make this, all four of you?"

"We had to call Rose a couple of times for instructions. And we skipped the olive oil."

"So your sister knows about the dinner." Lia dabbed her lips with a paper napkin. "Want to tell me what this is about?"

"Later."

Oh, boy. Lia tried to eat, but swallowing was difficult. She drank more wine than usual and started to get a little high. Her face was flushed.

In the house, her darling offspring were bickering back and forth. Lia looked over at Jake and said waggishly, "Romantic dinner with kids."

He arched an eyebrow. "I could get used to it."

"You're nuts. I would have pegged you for a dedicated bachelor."

"I was for a long time."

"Weren't you ever in love?"

"Once."

"Me, too. Just once."

"Larry?"

"Yep. What about yours?"

Jake didn't answer.

She rearranged her remaining green beans. "If you can't trust me…"

"Cherise," he said grittily. "She was a cocktail waitress at a strip club. Had her eye on becoming a pole dancer. I met her when I was young and full of myself after being chosen for the Rangers. We eloped to Vegas one weekend. The marriage lasted eight months."

Lia took a minute to digest the surprising news. She'd never imagine Jake married. It was absurd to be jealous of a marriage that had broken up so many years ago, but she couldn't seem to help herself. "What happened?"

"I was sent off for Special Forces training. She found the separation too difficult and took comfort with someone else."

"I hate her," Lia said on pure impulse.

"Don't bother. I can't even remember her face."

He remembered the pain of having his heart broken, she thought. If he'd been half the man at twenty that he was now, he'd have taken his vows seriously. So seriously that he wouldn't enter into another marriage lightly.

Jake got up and paced across the grass. He unbuttoned his cuffs and pushed up the sleeves. "This isn't going the way it was supposed to."

"You made a lovely effort." Lia slapped at a mosquito. As the evening grew darker, more of the annoying insects were attracted to the lights and candle flames.

"There's still a cake to come."

She put aside her napkin. "Chocolate?"

"Of course."

"We could have it inside."

"And disappoint the kids? No." Frowning, Jake rubbed the back of his neck. "I should probably get this over with so we can relax."

Lia made a move to rise, but he was suddenly standing beside her. For a moment his knee seemed to buckle, but then he straightened again and said, "Lia."

"Yes, Jake." She stood. "We already did this once. I don't think a second time will change any—"

"Hear me out." He reached over to the chair where Kristen's stuffed animal had sat throughout dinner. Cuddlebunny fell over, and when Jake brought his hand back, he held a ring box.

Lia's eyes widened.

"I know you already gave me one answer," he said. "But it's been pointed out to me what an idiot I was about how I asked the question." He swallowed. "So I'm trying again. Only I'm not very good at, you know, being romantic. I'm hoping you'll reconsider anyway."

"I can't do this now." She was panicking. "Let's go inside."

He snapped open the little box. "We're not going anywhere until you answer."

She looked at the ring. A simple diamond band, half the size of the one Larry had been so proud to show off. This one was a ring for *her* to wear with pride.

What am I thinking? I can't marry Jake. He doesn't love me.

But he cares. And if he did come to love me, it would be for real.

A sound made her turn. The kids had come outside. Sam was holding a cake plate. The cake was lopsided, the crooked layers showing through a skimpy coat of chocolate icing. Lia felt her heart pounding. *They want me to say yes. Even Samantha.*

She looked at Jake and was astonished. He was nervous, too!

Lia set aside the jitters. She tried to think rationally.

Rose would be her sister-in-law.

They'd have a home.

Her case for custody would be strengthened considerably.

Even Larry might be neutralized, if Jake was right.

Every reason in the world to say yes—except that she'd be risking her heart. But she'd never put her own needs above the family's. Why start now?

Jake pulled out the ring. "Marry me, Lia."

She looked at the kids. "What do you think?"

"Yes!" shouted Kristen, standing on her toes.

After pushing up his glasses, Howie nodded, as solemn as a little soldier. But Lia could see that he was practically swollen with anticipation.

Sam was looking down at the cake. "Yeah, Mom. I mean, if you want. He's not too bad."

Lia touched the ring with the tip of her finger. Jake started to slide it on, but she stopped him. "I haven't said yes yet. But you're not too bad." Not bad at all. "So I think…"

She closed her eyes, said a short prayer, tried to take a deep breath and got stuck halfway through. She poked out her finger before she could change her mind. With her eyes still closed, she said, "Yes, I'll marry you."

Jake waited until her lids popped open. Then he looked deep into her eyes and put the ring on her finger. "Good," he said in the steady voice she loved. Short and to the point.

Howie and Kristen were jumping up and down in celebration. Lia closed her eyes again and sort of slithered into Jake's arms. Considering their audience, his kiss was relatively chaste—but thrilling enough for her to add a couple of hundred points to the plus column.

Good, she thought, certain that she'd made the right decision.

"I DON'T KNOW IF I MADE the right decision," Lia confessed a few days later. She turned the ring on her finger. "Pass the syrup, 'cause I'm waffling like crazy."

Tess and Beth were leading the way through downtown Alouette, several strides ahead. Lia considered them friends, but she hadn't shared more than the rudimentary explanation of how she'd fled from her ex-husband and decided to marry Jake on short notice. They may have put the two facts together, because they'd accepted the hasty marriage without question.

Lia knew that Rose would understand her doubts, even though the groom was her brother. She'd seen Lia struggle up from rock bottom.

"Let's figure it out," Rose said, linking arms. She wore movie-star sunglasses with a tank top and frayed jeans shorts. "What's bothering you most?"

"Aside from the fact that I'm risking my kids' future on a quickie wedding?"

"We could put it off."

Lia said no. She and Jake had decided that there was no reason to delay other than placating public opinion. Private opinion also. They'd gone to visit his mother to give her the news. Maxine Robbin had not been a happy woman, clearly feeling that her position in the family home had been usurped.

"The longer we take, the more doubts I'll have," Lia said.

"But if you're that doubtful…"

"I'm not." Lia heard her firm response and realized that she'd spoken without thinking. Despite her worries, a big part of her was still certain about marrying Jake. "It's natural to be hesitant. Cold feet, right?"

Rose seemed concerned, but she smiled. "Then let's get a pedicure for those cold feet of yours so at least they'll look pretty."

Beth pulled open the door of a small salon called the Kute Kut. "Get moving, gals. Lia's having the works." Since there would be no bridal shower, Tess and Beth had announced that they were giving Lia a makeover appointment for a bridal gift.

"I need it, hmm?" Lia looked at the storefront, saw her reflection in the window and wanted to cringe. She hadn't been inside a salon for a few years, not even for a haircut. When her hair grew past her shoulders, she snipped the ends.

"Oh, no, you're very pretty," Tess said. She was trim and bright. Her clothes never wrinkled. Lia could have resented her if her intentions weren't so sincere. "But every woman should be head-to-toe beautiful for her wedding."

Lia touched her hair. What did Jake see in her? The way he looked at her made her feel beautiful—even if she had sticky ice cream hair or a red nose from crying. She'd forgotten that feeling, it had been so long.

"Let's go," she said, keeping hold of Rose so she wouldn't veer away at the last second. Rose's limited salon experience made Lia seem high-maintenance.

Within minutes, Lia was staring up at the ceiling with her head in the shampoo sink. The plan was color and a cut. A protesting Rose had been buttonholed by the manicurist. Beth's hair was being trimmed, and

Tess was debating the merits of a facial versus a manicure.

The stylist tilted Lia upright and drew a comb through her hair. "A natural blonde. You must be Scandinavian."

"My mother's family was from Norway."

"This is Finn country," said the manicurist, an unnatural blonde named Gloria Kevanen. Lia recognized her as Jeremy's mother. She'd been at that humiliating meeting with the sheriff and had babbled about bad influences while staring daggers at Sam.

"Where's your girl? Samantha, isn't it?" Gloria screwed up her snub nose. "She should be here. You don't want blue-streaked hair and chippy nails in the wedding party."

"There won't be a wedding party," Lia said coolly. "Only a justice of the peace." Truthfully, getting married with a JP again gave her a qualm. *Superstition,* she'd imagined Jake saying, so she hadn't spoken up.

Not the best beginning.

"What a shame," Gloria said. "I s'pose, under the circumstances…" She sent an arch look at the stylist, who frowned.

Rose yanked her hand out of Gloria's. "There are no circumstances."

"Touchy." Gloria waved a rosewood stick. "Gosh, I remember how many girls were after Jake back in high school. There are still some who'd love to get him down the aisle."

"Too bad Lia sashayed in and managed a coup in only a couple of weeks," Beth teased.

Gloria's gaze scraped over Lia. "You must be real special."

"She is," Tess said, ever loyal.

Lia gave her a grateful look.

Gloria wasn't finished. "You do get around, Lia. The Berry Dairy, the library, the Robbins' cottages, the police station. About the only place you haven't shown up is the Cedar Swamp. Did you know Jake goes there?"

"What's the Cedar Swamp?" Lia asked in spite of herself.

"One of the local bars," Beth explained.

"Jake's no drinker." Rose was huffy.

"Of course not," Gloria said soothingly. "I'm sure he's nothing like Black Jack."

Viper. As the stylist worked on Lia's hair, applying foil to different sections, she made herself put Gloria the manicurist out of her mind and relax. She wasn't worried about Jake in that respect. In fact, she wasn't worried about him at all.

Tess guided the conversation in another direction, and Lia's thoughts drifted. Maybe after she was dolled up, looking like a fresh young bride again, Jake wouldn't be able to stop himself from falling in love with her.

CHAPTER FOURTEEN

THE NIGHT BEFORE THE wedding, Lia had a craving to see Jake. She waited until Howie and Kristen were in bed, then stepped into her flip-flops.

Sam was up, reading a library book. Lia leaned over the chair to drop a kiss on her daughter's head. She said she was going next door. "You're all right with this, aren't you? The wedding and all. I know it's kind of sudden."

Except for being quiet and broody, Sam had taken her punishment for the vandalism well. She was even handling being grounded from hanging out with Danny and the others. Lia almost dared to believe that they'd turned a corner and life would be less bumpy from here on out, even if they had to travel in the Grudge.

"I'm okay." Sam glanced up. In addition to changing her hair, she'd been wearing less of the gaudy makeup the past few days and looked the prettier for it. More like a fourteen-year-old, although she wouldn't want to hear that. She claimed she'd run out of her favorite mascara. Lia thought the change was an effort at good behavior.

"Are you okay?" Sam asked.

"Me? I'm fine." Lia was a bit startled to be asked about herself by her self-involved teenager. That didn't happen too often.

Sam had something on her mind. Finally she blurted it out. "Are you only marrying Jake because of Dad?"

"What do you mean?"

"To keep him from getting custody. Like, I don't want to live with Dad, but I don't want you to have to get married, either."

Lia kneeled beside the chair. "I thought you wanted to go back to Cadillac."

Sam's mouth puckered. "I guess…not as much."

"I'm glad, honey. I want you here. Even when you're giving me trouble."

"Well, then, is that why you're marrying Jake— because I caused so much trouble?"

Lia tried to be honest with her children when she could, particularly Sam. "It's not because of you, Sam. But custody is part of my decision. Judges tend to look favorably on the parent who can provide best, in a stable environment." Lia had barely clung to custody previously. Without Jake standing beside her, she was sure to lose it the next time.

"Oh, Mom."

"Wait. The main thing is that I think Jake will be good for all of us, even if there is no custody fight. He already has been." *The truth,* she thought. *Tell it to yourself, too.* "And, well, I'm also kind of in love with him. I want to marry Jake for me."

"Really, truly?" Sam seemed amazed. "But he's not like Dad at all. He wears camouflage like he's still in the Army and he hunts and fishes. Did you see all the dead fish and deer heads in his house? It's gross. I might become a vegetarian."

Lia withheld her laugh. Sam was being serious, and she didn't want to ruin the moment. "I know what you mean, honey. But those are outward aspects of his character. What counts is the kind of man he is inside."

The kind who couldn't say he loved them but had already showed it in a dozen ways. Who wouldn't go down on one knee when proposing but would die protecting her and the kids.

That's good enough for me. It has to be.

"I guess." Sam's thumb was rifling the pages of her book.

"Were you still hoping I'd go back to your dad?"

Sam shrugged. "That's baby stuff."

"It wouldn't have happened, you know, even without Jake in the picture." Lia stood. "I shouldn't be long, but don't stay up too late if I am."

She left the cottage and hurried next door, thinking of Tess and Rose and Beth and Claire, all cozy at home with their husbands. She might have that with Jake, but suddenly there seemed so much they hadn't discussed. Trophy fish were the least of her concerns.

Did she knock? Ring the bell? She hadn't had time to think of herself as fiancée, let alone consider matters of etiquette.

Lia let herself in. Jake was at the dining room table, hunched over a notebook. "C'mere. I want to show you something."

C'mere? One day, when his habits became less adorable, she would have to talk to him about that.

"What are you doing?"

"Planning our house."

"I thought we'd live here."

"We will, but it's too small. Only the two bedrooms plus the attic. I was thinking I could build an addition between the two houses, connect them. We'd have another eight hundred square feet, all told. The cottage you're in now could become the master suite."

Lia looked over his drawings. "Wow. You've really been thinking about this." The space issue had also been on her mind ever since she'd realized that his mother expected to return and live with them. The chance of that had given her major pause, but she'd decided that taking Jake as a husband meant accepting the bad with the good.

"I'll make the attic over for Howie. Putting in a couple of dormer windows will open it up."

"He would love that. He's been so good about sharing tight quarters with three females that I'd like to do something special for him." Lia stared at Jake's shoulders, so broad they stretched his Army camou-flage T-shirt taut. His arms were deeply tanned. His nape and nose were lightly sunburned. He had worked on property upkeep all day, making the place present-able for the short list of their wedding guests.

"You're a little sunburned. I'll go find the moisturizing cream." The burn wasn't all that bad, but her fingers tingled at the thought of getting to touch him.

She went into the bathroom and located a tube of lotion. Only a small amount remained, but there was more at her house. Howie and Kristen had been outdoors so often the past several weeks that they'd slowly turned brown as chestnuts despite their fair coloring.

Lia looked in the mirror. She looked a lot better, especially since her appointment at the Kute Kut. Her hair was light and wavy, her eyes clearer and brighter. Her skin no longer had a pasty hue. Tonight, though, the rosy color in her cheeks wasn't from getting too much sun.

She jumped when Jake appeared behind her. "You scared me."

He lifted a foot. "No shoes."

She showed him the almost empty tube. "We'll have to stretch it."

"I'm fine. I don't need no stinkin' sunburn cream."

"Don't play tough with me. You know you want it."

His eyes ignited. Her blush became even rosier.

They'd shared only a few kisses in the past week. The lack of a dating and courtship period made everything strange. She was hoping she'd know how to handle the wedding night when the time came. He hadn't mentioned the issue since the first time, but she remembered very well that he expected consummation.

Jake walked into his bedroom, pulling off the T-shirt as he went. Lia followed and tentatively poked her head into the room. She'd never been in his room.

The bedroom was small and spartan, the thick stone walls and low ceiling containing only a bureau with an oval mirror, a wooden chair that doubled as a nightstand and an old-fashioned iron bedstead with a mattress laid atop the springs. A row of antlers mounted to plaques was the lone wall decoration. Thankfully no nightmares of taxidermy. Personal possessions amounted to several pairs of shoes and boots lined up under the bed, a row of books on the bureau and a wallet laid beside an ironstone bowl filled with pinecones.

Lia smiled at that. "Kristen Rose and her nickels?"

"She wants me to keep them all. I pitch a few into the woods when she's not looking." Jake sat on the edge of the bed, his feet planted wide. He put his elbows on his knees and looked at her expectantly.

Her pulse was fast and hard. She slid into the room like melted butter and climbed onto the bed to kneel behind him. His broad back formed a muscled triangle. She squeezed out a dollop of cream and let her hands follow the angles.

"I'm not burned there," Jake said. "But don't stop."

He was right. Faint tan lines ringed his shoulders and neck, but he went without a shirt often enough that even the paler section of skin was toasted with warm color.

She stroked the cream across his nape. He made a sound of pleasure. "Feels cool."

"Your shoulders are a little red." She skimmed them with her greased fingertips.

She was hovering behind him. He asked, "What about my nose?" and leaned backward to offer it. Their bodies met, and she barely had time to register the sensation of his warm skin pressed against her before he'd turned and lowered her to the bed. His face was inches from hers. "Here's my nose."

She untangled an arm and rubbed the remaining cream on his nose. The tube was lost, but then she didn't care anymore because red-hot suddenly seemed exactly the right temperature.

He gazed at her from beneath lazy lids. "Thank you."

"Thank you for the house," she replied and kissed the tip of his greased nose.

"Thank you for agreeing to marry me." He kissed her mouth.

"Thank you for asking." She kissed him back.

"Thank you for the wedding night—in advance." With a low rumbling chuckle, he went to kiss her, then stopped. "What's wrong?"

"Nothing."

"Honesty, Lia."

She squirmed beneath him. "All right. I feel kind of strange about the wedding night. It's as if I'm jumping into bed with a guy on the first date, and I've never done that in my life."

Jake lifted up onto his elbows. "Some first date."

"I know. Don't worry, I'll seal the deal. This is only bridal jitters."

"You'll seal the deal, huh?"

She scrunched her nose. Wasn't that the way he wanted it?

Trying again to keep it on the level he preferred, she tried again. "What I meant was that I will perform my marital duties."

He rolled onto his side. "Yeah, that's better."

"You're the one who asked for full conjugal rights even though we're not in—in a normal situation."

"It's not abnormal, either."

She rubbed her fingers together. "No, and I never said that it was."

"'Full conjugal rights,'" he quoted.

"I was trying to be unemotional—for your sake."

"Don't do things for my sake, okay? Say what you mean."

"I'm trying to." With Larry, she'd had to watch every word because she never knew what would set him off on a tirade. "I said I felt strange about this."

"Yeah." Jake put his hand beneath her rib cage, fingers spread. Her shirt had pulled loose of the waistband of her shorts, and the inside of his wrist touched her navel like a lightning strike. "There doesn't have to be sex right away. We can wait as long as it takes for you to feel comfortable."

"Oh. Okay." She relaxed her neck so her head fell against the pillow. *Guess what? I'm comfortable.*

Jake's slightly lopsided grin made a slow appearance. "I might turn into a grizzly bear if it takes too long. But no rush."

She laughed, thinking how good it was to have a man who kept a sense of humor even when the discussion turned a little testy. "I'll spread you some honey in the meantime."

"Like now?"

He kissed her again, with a deliberate, sensual ease. For a man accustomed to barracks, rough conditions and backcountry expeditions, he had a gentle touch. A tongue both sweet and firm. Her arms wound around his shoulders and she luxuriated in the masculine breadth and length of him. She started to believe that they would have many nights like this—long, cozy nights under a quilt, desire like a river, sometimes coursing, sometimes meandering, forever changing yet always there.

He put his face in her hair and inhaled. "You smell great." His lips traced her ear. "Your hair is the color of creamy butter." He nipped. "And that's the end of my attempt at froufrou poetry."

She pretended to pout. "What about my eyes? Don't they flash like sapphires?"

"More like the river on a sunny day."

She loosened her arms to pull back and look in his eyes. "I bet you say that to all the girls."

He moved his head from side to side. *No.*

She ran her fingers over his tattoos. "What about RLTW?" *Rita Lynn Tiffany Winona...*

"Rangers Lead the Way. It's our slogan. But maybe it can work for you and me, too." His eyes were deep and dark as he kissed her. "Just call my name. I will always be there for you."

Outside, the owls were calling back and forth from the tops of the trees, no longer alone. Lia sighed with pleasure. Her heart sang, *Jake, Jake, Jake* as she snuggled in his arms. This was courtship. She didn't need twenty staid dinner dates and a dozen movie tickets and a night at the opera to make up her mind. Jake, the stubborn son of a gun, was it.

She already knew this: declarations of love from the wrong man added up to nothing. For the right man, she could wait.

IT WASN'T A GARDEN wedding. It was a backyard wedding. A barely civilized backyard, even with Jake's precision lawn mowing and Howie's diligence with the rake. Pine needles stuck to the guests' shoes, but most of them wore sandals or sneakers anyway. The seating was a motley collection of lawn chairs. No florist had touched the bouquets of Queen Anne's lace and daisies. Every guest brought a potluck dish. There was even a Lutheran pastor, who'd been enlisted after Jake's mother nixed the justice of the peace by wondering, repeatedly, if such a marriage counted outside of a courthouse. Nobody mentioned to her that they also lacked a church.

Jake strolled around the cottages trying to appear

nonchalant. Evan, the newlywed, came up and asked which was worse—waiting for the ceremony or facing artillery fire. Jake loosened the knot in his tie.

Women were continually running in and out of Lia's cottage, shouting things like, "A needle" and "Pink!" Sam flew out the door in a dress, trailing ribbons and petals. She tore a circlet of flowers off her head, raised her arm to toss it to the ground, then saw Jake watching. She glared. He stared. She slapped the thing back on her head and skulked off to sit with Danny.

The pastor tried to engage Jake in conversation, mentioning church attendance, Sunday school, solid foundations. Jake nodded, then nodded some more. He thought of pediatricians, Little League, Halloween costumes and braces. Had he believed that gaining a ready-made family would be simple? Apparently so.

Maxine Robbin held court in the front row, ensconced in a wheelchair with a nasal tube in place and a tank of oxygen nearby. Using a high-pitched drone that carried across the yard, she said that while Lia seemed like a fine woman despite the arrest, she had her doubts about the girl with glitter nail polish. Howie gained favor by fetching and carrying for his new step-grandma Maxine—a drink of water, the lace handkerchief she'd left in the top drawer of her bureau, a photo of Jackson Robbin Sr. to hold in her lap so he could "attend" the wedding.

They hadn't planned for music or a processional.

Right when Jake was on the edge of bolting for the river and a getaway kayak, a group of women emerged from the cottage, Lia among them.

He stood, poleaxed, while the rest of the world faded away. He'd known, of course, that Lia was pretty. And even prettier just lately, with her fine dandelion hair trimmed and shaped so it floated around her head like a halo.

This was different. She glowed. The colors of her simple dress—pink and yellow and white—were set off by a light tan. She was slim and graceful. There were flowers in her hair. Her face was solemn as she approached Jake, but when she smiled she lit him up inside like fireworks on the Fourth of July.

He took her hand and whispered in her ear. "Hey, beautiful. Let's get hitched."

LIA'S HANDS WERE trembling. She clutched a bouquet with one hand and Jake with the other. Pastor Mike Greenlee greeted them with beneficence and opened the ceremony by welcoming the guests. He spoke casually, skipping phrases like *We are gathered here,* as Jake and Lia had requested.

"Before we begin the vows, I suppose I should ask if anyone has reason to object to this wedding?" The pastor paused dramatically and cocked his head in a listening posture. Except for the hum of a car driving by on Blackbear Road, there was silence. Pastor Greenlee chuckled. "Didn't think so." He opened his book.

Maxine wheezed. She gave a delicate cough, then another. Jake and Lia turned. Maxine waved her handkerchief in the air. "Never mind me. Proceed with the ceremony."

Jake looked at Lia. "Whew."

She squeezed his hand, but she couldn't quite stop trembling. She dug her flat sandal heels into the ground.

"All right then." Pastor Mike opened the book again and searched for his lost spot. "Here we go."

The distinct sound of a car driving down the sloping driveway stopped him. "Ah. We have a late arrival."

Guests had parked their vehicles all along the drive, under the trees. To find a spot, the latecomer would have to pull up practically on the doorstep.

The car braked hard, only feet away from plowing into the guests, some of whom had risen in alarm.

Jake gave Lia a quick glance. He took a few steps toward the unfamiliar car. "What the—?"

Lia stared. The car door opened. A tall man with thinning sandy-colored hair unfolded himself from the driver's seat. He stared in astonishment at the gathering before him, his jaw hanging open.

Dizziness washed over Lia. The trembling that had receded swept back in. She dropped her bouquet, reaching for Jake's hand.

He turned back to her, reading her expression even before she could get her tongue to work. She held onto his arm. "That—that—that's Larry."

Kristen put her hand up by her mouth. Her clear voice piped above the murmuring of the guests. "Daddy?"

Larry came around the car, his arms spreading wide. "Krissy, Howie, Samantha. I've come to take you home."

CHAPTER FIFTEEN

JAKE GREW BEFORE LIA'S eyes. At least she thought he did. He stood taller. His muscles got bigger. His hands opened wide, then closed into clenched fists. Indignation simmered, on the verge of a boiling steam.

She darted past him and swept Kristen up in her arms. "Larry, my God. What are you doing here?"

Her ex-husband surveyed the gathering, smugly enjoying the attention of having all eyes on him. After the first buzz of whispering, the guests had fallen silent. Waiting for the next development.

Lia shuddered. She wanted a life, not a soap opera.

Larry took his time, smoothing back the limp hair that had fallen across his forehead, tugging on his cuffs. Finally he answered. "I'm here for the kids you stole. What in hell are you doing?"

"Getting married," Jake declared in a booming voice. Heads swiveled toward him like tennis spectators. The answer was clearly a challenge.

"Let's stay calm." But Lia couldn't contain the tremor in her own voice. She clutched Kristen tighter, who threw her arm around her mother's neck, dangling

Cuddlebunny by one ear. "This isn't the way to settle custody, Larry. Talk to my lawyer."

"Lawyers," he sneered.

Jake advanced past Lia. They were walking the wrong way down the aisle. "We can call the cops instead."

Evan stood up, holding a cell phone. Rose popped up beside him, jutting a pugnacious chin. Then even timid little Lucy rose, big-eyed and clinging to Rose's hand.

Larry glanced at Evan before returning his eyes to Jake. His face was flushed and contorted with temper, a phenomenon that Lia had appeased a thousand times. But this time there was something different. Less bluster. A certain shiftiness in the way he moved his shoulders and put his hands in and out of his pockets. The intimidator was intimidated, and Jake hadn't even gotten serious yet.

Maybe he wouldn't have to. Lia put Kristen down near Sam and went to whisper to Jake. "Please don't ruin the wedding by making a scene."

His brows crawled upward. "Me?"

"You don't know Larry. Things will escalate if you don't back off."

"That's what you always did, right? Did it work?"

She shrugged, feeling helpless. Only hopelessness was worse.

Larry had restored his outrage. "Give me the kids, Lia. Then you can go back to your yokel wedding." He tossed a smirk in Jake's direction. "I don't know how she talked you into marriage, but you can have the ungrateful bitch. I'm done with her."

Lia had thought she was past allowing Larry's words to degrade her, but the same old humiliation returned like a slap in the face. She recoiled.

In a blink, Jake was up in Larry's face, a barely suppressed violence evident in every strained line of his body. "Never talk about her that way again." He didn't need to add an *or else*. The threat was clear. "You're not welcome here. Get out. Now."

Larry stepped back. "I'll go, but only with the kids."

"You can't have them."

Larry was a couple of inches taller than Jake, but he pushed his chin even higher. He liked to feel superior. "I'm their father."

"You don't have custody."

Larry scowled. "I'll get it."

Jake bumped him in the chest. His balled fists lifted slightly. "See you in court."

Larry retreated farther. "You'll see me, all right. I'll press charges against her. I'll put her in jail."

Lia flinched. If only she could run or hide or bury her face in her hands. She was used to watching Larry raging about every little thing that ticked him off, but she hated what was happening to Jake.

Out of the corner of her eye, she saw her kids' faces. Kristen's cheeks were shiny with tears. Howie was pale and cringing. Sam was starkly expressionless, taking it all in through skeptical eyes.

The pang in Lia's heart made her mad. *I can't stand by doing nothing.*

She inserted herself between Larry and Jake. Her intention was to prevent a fight. But when she looked into her former husband's arrogant face, she knew she couldn't let him get away with the usual rudeness and demands.

"Try to take the children, Larry, and it'll be your turn to be arrested." She attempted to think the way he did. "You'll lose your advantage in the courts."

"I'm owed a visitation."

She felt ferocious but cold and calm at the same time. "Don't worry. You'll get what's due."

His eyes narrowed. "Is that a threat?"

"I wouldn't threaten you in front of the kids." Even though he'd done it plenty to her. "For once, think of their feelings before your own."

"I am. They want to live with me."

"To be judged and belittled until they're as twisted as you? Over my dead body."

"You blew it when you took them, Lia." His smile gloated. "I've got leverage now."

"Then you should be pleased." Searching for a way to end the confrontation, she remembered how he'd prided himself on his ability to negotiate concessions. After he'd been promoted at work and begun making better money, his ego had grown. He'd often come home boasting of the deals he'd finagled.

Lia continued. "Larry, we're trying to have a wedding here. If you go away now without further incident, I may let you see the kids tomorrow." With supervision. She wouldn't let them out of her sight when he was around.

She'd thought that she was reaching him, but her last words touched off his temper. "You'll *let* me?" he snarled. "Since when do I allow you to make the decisions?"

"Never," she said quietly. "But it's time to start."

Jake was pressing against her from behind, still on the verge of taking a swing at Larry. She felt as if she were tiptoeing through land mines. Setting off either man would be cataclysmic.

Pastor Mike put a hand on Larry's shoulder. "Sir, these arguments are better settled in private. I can offer a counseling session—"

Larry brushed off the man like a fly. "Stuff it, Bible-thumper. I don't buy into your brand of crap." He had little faith in institutions, though he used them to his advantage when it was convenient.

Maxine Robbin gasped. "There's no call for such rudeness." A few murmurs agreed.

Larry sneered at her, too. "Tough nuts, you old bat."

"That's it." Jake grabbed Larry's arm, nearly tearing off the appendage as he hauled the man bodily toward his car.

Larry fumed and cursed about the manhandling, but he'd been caught unaware and wasn't able to regain his feet. Helpless, he was dragged across the grass.

Lia ran after them. "Jake! Please don't hurt him."

Jake threw Larry across the hood of his car and held him down with a handful of collar. "Can I trust you to drive out of here like a gentleman or do I have to put you in the back of my truck and take you for a nice long ride?"

Larry's limbs slithered in all directions as he slid away from Jake. He got to his feet, still belligerent but no longer willing to prolong the conflict. "Backwoods baboon," he muttered while tucking in his rumpled shirt. He flung the car door open and jammed himself behind the wheel. His mouth twisted from the venom that he'd had to swallow.

"This isn't over," he jeered as he shoved the key into the ignition. "Payback's a bitch."

"Not when the bastard's balls are cut off," Jake muttered. He was breathing hard, infused with so much rampaging testosterone that Lia could sense it oozing from his pores. She was not quite sure how to react.

Larry gunned the engine. Jake slammed a hand on the hood. He hunched down to glare through the windshield.

"Step back," Lia pleaded. She gripped Jake's arm to drag him away. It was like trying to move a boulder. She tugged ineffectually.

His eyes were bloodshot. He looked at her as if he didn't know who she was.

She shivered. "Please, Jake."

He gave his head a vigorous shake, and when he met

her eyes the second time, she knew that he'd come back to her. He straightened with a snap and moved away from the car.

Larry put the vehicle in Reverse and roared down the driveway in a cloud of dirt and pine needles, crunching pinecones under the tires and sending small sticks and stones bouncing off the wedding guests' autos. Once the car hit Blackbear Road, he put it in drive and took off with a squeal of rubber on asphalt.

A deathly silence descended. Lia felt little relief. Larry would be back. He always came back.

She straightened her dress. Smoothed her hair. She wasn't ready to face the stunned guests. Jake, either. Her emotions were in turmoil.

He blew out a breath and yanked his tie open. She felt his gaze on her, warily. "Look, I'm sorry if I was too harsh. But guys like that—they're bullies. They don't listen to reason. You have to show them who's boss. Rub their noses in it and they don't come back."

Lia's head was down. "Larry always comes back."

"Not with me around."

"Uh-huh."

"Lia…" Jake pressed his palm to her cheek, trying to get her to raise her face and look at him. "I'm sorry."

She pulled away from the touch she'd come to crave. Everything was tainted now. "Larry used to apologize, too, afterward."

"Don't confuse me with that dirtbag."

She hesitated before nodding. "I know. You're no

dirtbag." But she was no longer quite as certain about who he was, either.

"Should we put this off or, uh…" Jake's voice got deep and gravelly. "Do you want to go through with the wedding?"

Lia looked at Pastor Mike smiling encouragement. Evan and Rose concerned yet trying not to appear flustered. One or two of the other guests were shocked and whispering, but most gave her signs that she should come back and go on as if nothing had happened.

Lia almost believed that she could. Until she looked at the peaked, withdrawn, shell-shocked faces of her children.

Enough.

Jake was becoming alarmed. "Lia, tell me that you still want to marry me."

A sob rose in her throat so sharp it seemed to cut her vocal cords. Hoarsely she said, "I don't. I don't want to marry you," and whirled around to flee, not wanting to watch as Jake realized he was being jilted at the altar.

THE GUESTS MILLED around, uncertain how to proceed. Jake saw Rose motion for him to go after Lia. He raised his hands, suddenly feeling utterly inadequate. How could he justify himself? He'd lost his temper and, just like that, he'd lost his bride.

Sam broke away from the group and took off in the same direction as her mother. He looked after her, wanting to follow but knowing he shouldn't unless he was ready to tell Lia what she needed to hear.

But could he? In Jake's moment of doubt, there seemed no more denying that he was Black Jack's son through and through, just another brawler who'd failed himself and the people he loved.

Rose came forward. Everyone else looked at him as if he might have popped a blood vessel, but his sister was made of sterner stuff. "Well, that was quite a show."

"Was it really bad?"

"A little shocking, but could have been worse. Actually, I'm surprised the guests didn't cheer when you tossed Larry across the car."

Jake couldn't smile, even though he'd relished the moment. "I had to do it."

"Maybe."

"Lia's done with me."

"Maybe not."

"You saw her. I scared her."

"Yeah, you did. But you have to understand— because of the way Larry treated her, she's more sensitive to yelling and aggression than, say, me. Let her calm down and then see what she decides."

Jake put his head in his hands, wishing there was a way to crush the self-doubt out of it. His heart pounded like a drum from the adrenaline. He would have sworn that he'd learned how to control his instinct for aggression. Could Lia possibly understand that he'd only done it for her sake?

"Larry deserved it." Rose put her hand on one of Jake's arms and made him lower them. "Don't beat yourself up for getting a little hotheaded."

He shook off the sympathy. He didn't deserve it.

"It's not the end of the world," Evan said, joining them.

"Only the end of the wedding." Jake looked bleakly at the small group who'd come to celebrate nuptials, not a bare-knuckle brawl. "What do we do about the guests?"

"Oh, Jake." Rose grimaced. "Don't give up so soon. Are you sure the wedding's off?"

"You heard her. Everyone heard her. I might as well send them home."

"Hold on for a few minutes, okay? I'll go and mingle to test the mood."

Jake shrugged. He no longer cared. The day that had begun with such bright promise had turned into hopeless gloom.

LIA DIDN'T KNOW WHERE to go. The cottages were Jake's domain. She needed a haven of her own.

The Grudge. The battered old Impala wouldn't fail her this time. She'd backed it into a make-do parking space just past the cottage, half hidden under the evergreen boughs. She ducked under them to reach the driver's side. The door hinges that used to screech so horribly had been oiled—Jake's doing. Luckily she'd left the key in the ignition.

She put her fingers on the key but didn't turn it.

Where would she go? Running away hadn't worked out so well the last time she'd tried it.

The point was debatable. Sure, she'd been arrested. But she'd also met Jake.

Who'd been five minutes away from becoming her husband.

Lia pounded the steering wheel in frustration. "Damn you, Larry." He'd managed to ruin her happiness once again.

The passenger door opened. Lia's heart leaped, but it was Samantha, sliding into the seat with a worried look on her face. "Are you okay, Mom?"

Lia took inventory of a multitude of emotions. She was mad, she was disappointed, she was brokenhearted. "I'm mortified," she blurted, picking the least of her reactions. "Imagine what the guests are thinking. First you're arrested, then I'm arrested, then Jake's marrying me, then I'm not marrying him." She groaned. "What a complete mess."

"You left out Dad."

"Him—" Lia cut off the vitriol she wanted to heap on Larry's head. Not to his daughter.

Sam picked at her purple glitter nail polish. "I guess he sort of ruined the wedding."

"Sort of. Yeah." Lia sensed her daughter's conflicted feelings. "Tell me the truth, Sam. Was I wrong? Do you still think about living with your father?"

"I'd go," Sam said. Lia's heart sank. "But only if that meant he wouldn't bother you anymore."

"Oh, sweetie." They hugged. "I'd never ask you to do that for me, but I appreciate the offer." Lia brushed her fingers through Sam's hair and straightened the lopsided circlet of flowers that Lucy had been so proud of creating for the wedding. Her tough little girl looked so forlorn.

Damn you, Larry. Lia sat back and held the wheel in a death grip. She wanted to scream and honk the horn and throw things. "I'm sorry for saying it, Sam, but I despise Larry for putting you between us. You shouldn't have to make a choice."

"I can deal."

Lia gave a mirthless laugh. "I wish I could."

After a short silence, Sam asked tentatively, "Why don't you want to marry Jake? Yesterday you said you loved him."

"I realized that we were, uh, rushing into it, I suppose you'd say. When I saw him go after your dad, well…"

Jake had said he had a temper, but it had always been so well hidden she'd found the worrisome trait all too easy to forget about. Especially compared to Larry, who'd had no compunction about letting her know the instant he was in an ugly mood.

Seeing Jake's ire rise so quickly had devastated her image of the man she'd believed him to be. When he'd asked if she still wanted to marry him, she'd realized with a cold dread that she might be making the same mistake twice.

"I thought it was really kind of wicked-cool," Sam said. "But then I felt sorry for Dad." She glanced at Lia. "You were afraid that Jake would hurt him."

"The scene was nasty enough without real violence." Actually, Lia hadn't cared so much about what happened to Larry as she'd been afraid of Jake facing charges for beating her ex-husband to a pulp.

"Jake was like the Incredible Hulk."

"That's not good."

"It was kind of scary." Sam rolled down her window and stuck an elbow outside. "Maybe we should pack up and go."

"Go?" Lia couldn't bring herself to fathom the idea.

"I mean, it's obvious that all men are jerks, right? Even Jake."

"I don't—" *Want to go.* Lia licked her dry lips. "I don't know where we'd go. No, that's not what I meant. I don't want to go. I want to get married."

"Cripes, Mom. To Jake? What's the point? You might as well have stayed with Dad."

"Jake's not like your father. You've got to see that, Sam." Lia listened to her own words. *Take them to heart,* she told herself. *Believe in Jake again.*

"But why do you have to marry him? You don't need him, do you, Mom? When we left Cadillac, you said you were going to be an independent woman and take care of us by yourself." Sam stuck her fist under her chin. "I liked it when we were on the road together. Even if it was in the Grudge, with Howie counting miles and Krissy having to pee all the time."

"I remember." Lia wondered if she'd given up on herself too soon. For all that she felt for Jake, would the problems outweigh the pluses? Seeking his protection might not be setting the right kind of example for her kids.

Sam was already too confused. She was leery of her father. Alternately impressed and frightened by Jake's fierce character. Certainly she was already way too cynical about marriage and men. And she was looking to Lia to show the way.

"Samantha, my sweet-'n'-sour girl." Big breath. "I know you were too young to remember, but there was a time that your father and I loved each other. We started out with good intentions. Yes, we 'had' to get married and that was rough for a while, especially because my parents had a hard time getting past their disappointment in me. But we had a darling baby girl and we were young and in love, and for a while…" Too brief, it seemed now. "For a time, we had a happy marriage."

Lia looped an arm around her daughter. She touched her head to Sam's. "I'm sorry that I haven't been able to show you what a good marriage is all about. Howie and Kristen, too."

Sam squirmed. "Mom, you're so cheesy."

"It's been a rough day. Let me have my little Hallmark moment."

Sam didn't pull away. They sat looking toward their small cottage and the short stretch of land between it and the main house. Jake had begun work on clearing the area, preparing to build the addition.

The connection, Lia thought.

And she'd made one at last.

The way to set an example for Sam—and prove her own worth to herself—was not in refusing the hand that Jake offered. While being strong enough to stand on her own was a vital lesson for any woman, there was also courage and honor in being able to accept help when it was needed. Her greatest strength might come in teaching her children how to love without fear. And with their entire hearts.

JAKE STOOD HIDDEN among the pine trees, listening to the conversation. He remained crestfallen but was slowly gaining determination not to give up so easily. Even when Lia seemed to be saying that any marriage, even a happy one, can go sour. The melancholy apology to Sam sounded as if she doubted she'd be in a good marriage anytime soon.

Despite that, his stubbornness had kicked in. He might have to court her. Pull out all the romantic stops. Maybe the kids would help him again, although he had his doubts about Sam.

If he got another chance to romance Lia, he wouldn't stop short. He'd go all the way.

"Almost all of my friends' parents are divorced,"

Sam said. "I don't think there are any happy marriages."

"Of course there are." Lia sounded shocked but doubtful. "What about Evan and Rose?"

"Only newlyweds."

Lia mumbled other names, people Jake didn't know. Sam kept shooting her down.

"Would you and Jake have been happy?" Sam asked, and he thought for a couple of seconds that he was back in the Middle East amid a percussion blast. His hearing went out, the world got small and silent, then expanded at the speed of sound with Lia's answer.

"I think so."

He began to hope again.

"But maybe not," Sam speculated.

"There are no guarantees. We love—we like and respect each other. That's a good place to start."

Didn't sound like enough, even to Jake.

They were emerging from the car, Sam first. "Then how come you're not marrying him?"

Lia climbed out. She slammed the door, gave the rattletrap vehicle a pat and sighed. "It's complicated."

Jake stepped out of the trees. "It doesn't have to be complicated."

He'd startled her. She put her hand over her mouth and turned a very bridal shade of pink. "Were you eavesdropping on us?"

"It was an interesting conversation."

"Jake," she said. Only that. He waited for more, but

she simply gestured in an I-don't-know-what-to-say way.

"Are you having second thoughts, Lia?"

"Yes, and second thoughts about my second thoughts, too. But I still don't know if we should…" She shook her head sorrowfully, and a few of the less jaunty flower petals fluttered free.

"Is it because I lost my temper?"

"That's part of it."

He went to her, reaching for her hands. She let him take them. He recognized the trust in her eyes even before he spoke his piece. "I would never raise a hand to you or the kids. I might raise my voice—I can't promise I'll never get mad enough to do that. But it would be on rare occasions, I hope." His voice was getting stuck in his throat. "I'm very aware that I need to watch my temper, you know. I grew up with a man who let it rip. I wouldn't do that to you or Howie or Kristen. Or Sam." He glanced at Sam, who was nibbling at her nail while she watched them. "We might argue about Sam's discipline. I'm not running *Mister Rogers' Neighborhood,* either."

"Great," muttered Sam, but Jake was waiting to hear from Lia.

She smiled. "I know all that."

"What about—" he motioned with his head "—back there?"

"Larry? That shocked me. And I won't say it doesn't worry me a little. What about when he comes back? I don't want to be collecting you from jail every time Larry provokes you."

"Believe me, now that Larry knows he can't push you around, he won't be a problem. At least not such a big one."

"I'd love to believe you. I don't know if I should."

"Time will tell."

Lia closed her eyes and moved a little closer. She squeezed his hands. "I may have spoken too fast saying that I wouldn't marry you," she offered in a hesitant voice. "I needed a little time to think this through. Talking to Sam made me realize that I do need to stand up for myself. Because if I run away instead, I'll be throwing away my best chance at happiness."

"Mo-om." Sam seemed to be confounded. "You said—"

"Sam, I can be a strong, independent woman and still be married. Maybe not in my first marriage, but in my second…" Lia looked shyly at Jake, but when she saw his expression, her eyes became bright and her smile turned bold. "I'm going to get it right this time. Jake might find himself with more woman than he can handle."

He raised his brows. "I hope so."

Lia only smiled. She was waiting.

Jake didn't disappoint. His wounded pride crumbled away and he dropped to one knee. He knew others were watching and probably smiling indulgently at the sight of the wild man brought to his knees by a meek woman, but he concentrated on Lia's beautiful face. Her bountiful love.

"I'm only a humble guy who's not used to wearing my heart on my sleeve. But I love you, Lia, and will be a good husband to you and a father to your children. Tell me once more that you're game to marry me."

Lia's face was as bright as a North Country sky. "I'm game."

He jumped up and swooped her into his arms. The curious wedding guests, who'd wandered past the cottages and gathered nearby, broke out into applause and cheers. Kristin called, "Mommy!" and ran over to Lia and Jake. They picked her up between them, and those closest swore forever afterward that Black Jack's son blushed when a certain lop-eared stuffed rabbit kissed him on the mouth. He may have even smacked his lips and kissed the rabbit in return.

Howie began ringing the bell, and Pastor Mike threw up his hands. "Praise be! Let's have ourselves a wedding."

* * * * *

Turn the page for a sneak preview of
IF I'D NEVER KNOWN YOUR LOVE
by
Georgia Bockoven

From the brand-new series
Harlequin Everlasting Love
Every great love has a story to tell. ™

One year, five months and four days missing

There's no way for you to know this, Evan, but I haven't written to you for a few months. Actually, it's been almost a year. I had a hard time picking up a pen once more after we paid the second ransom and then received a letter saying it wasn't enough. I was so sure you were coming home that I took the kids along to Bogotá so they could fly home with you and me, something I swore I'd never do. I've fallen in love with Colombia and the people who've opened their hearts to me. But fear is a constant companion when I'm there. I won't ever expose our children to that kind of danger again.

I'm at a loss over what to do anymore, Evan. I've begged and pleaded and thrown temper tantrums with every official I can corner both here and at home. They've been incredibly tolerant and understanding, but in the end as ineffectual as the rest of us.

I try to imagine what your life is like now, what you do every day, what you're wearing, what you eat. I want to believe that the people who have you are misguided yet kind, that they treat you well. It's how I survive day to day. To think of you being mistreated hurts too much. If I picture you locked away somewhere and suffering, a weight descends on me that makes it almost impossible to get out of bed in the morning.

Your captors surely know you by now. They have to recognize what a good man you are. I imagine you working with their children, telling them that you have children, too, showing them the pictures you carry in your wallet. Can't the men who have you understand how much your children miss you? How can it not matter to them?

How can they keep you away from us all this time? Over and over, we've done what they asked. Are they oblivious to the depth of their cruelty? What kind of people are they that they don't care?

I used to keep a calendar beside our bed next to the peach rose you picked for me before you left. Every night I marked another day, counting how many you'd been gone. I don't do that any longer. I don't want to be reminded of all the days we'll never get back.

When I can't sleep at night, I tell you about my day. I imagine you hearing me and smiling over the details that make up my life now. I never tell you how defeated I feel at moments or how hard I work to hide it from everyone for fear they will see it as a reason to stop believing you are coming home to us.

And I couldn't tell you about the lump I found in my breast and how difficult it was going through all the tests without you here to lean on. The lump was benign—the process reaching that diagnosis utterly terrifying. I couldn't stop thinking about what would happen to Shelly and Jason if something happened to me.

We need you to come home.

I'm worn down with missing you.

I'm going to read this tomorrow and will probably tear it up or burn it in the fireplace. I don't want you to get the idea I ever doubted what I was doing to free you or thought the work a burden. I would gladly spend the rest of my life at it, even if, in the end, we only had one day together.

You are my life, Evan.

I will love you forever.

* * * * *

Don't miss this deeply moving
Harlequin Everlasting Love story
about a woman's struggle to bring back
her kidnapped husband from Colombia
and her turmoil over whether to let go, finally,
and welcome another man into her life.
IF I'D NEVER KNOWN YOUR LOVE
by Georgia Bockoven
is available March 27, 2007.

And also look for
THE NIGHT WE MET
by Tara Taylor Quinn,
a story about finding love
when you least expect it.

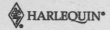

HARLEQUIN® *Romance.*

presents a brand-new trilogy by

PATRICIA THAYER

Rocky Mountain
B R I D E S

Three sisters come home to wed.

In April don't miss

Raising the Rancher's Family,

followed by

The Sheriff's Pregnant Wife,

on sale May 2007,

and

A Mother for the Tycoon's Child,

on sale June 2007.

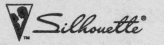

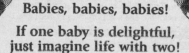
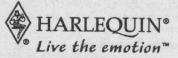

HARLEQUIN®

Super Romance®

COMING NEXT MONTH

#1410 ALL-AMERICAN FATHER • Anna DeStefano
Singles…with Kids
What's a single father to do when his twelve-year-old daughter is caught shoplifting a box of *expired* condoms? Derrick Cavennaugh sure doesn't know. He turns to Bailey Greenwood for help, but she's got troubles of her own....

#1411 EVERYTHING BUT THE BABY • Kathleen O'Brien
Having your fiancé do a runner is not the way any bride wants to spend her wedding day. Learning it's not the first time he's done it can give a woman a taste for revenge. And when a handsome man gives her the opportunity to do just that, who wouldn't take him up on it? Especially when it means spending more time with him.

#1412 REAL COWBOYS • Roz Denny Fox
Home on the Ranch
Kate Steele accepts a teaching job at a tiny school in rural Idaho. The widow of a rodeo star, she's determined to get her young son away from Texas and the influence of cowboys. Then she meets Ben Trueblood. He's the single father of one of her pupils— and a man she's determined to resist, no matter how attractive he is. Because he might call himself a buckaroo, but a cowboy by any other name…

#1413 RETURN TO TEXAS • Jean Brashear
Going Back
Once a half-wild boy fending for himself, Eli Wolverton is alive because Gabriela Navarro saved his life. They fell in love, yet Eli sent her away. Now she has returned to bury her father. He, like Eli's mother, died mysteriously in a fire—and Eli is accused of setting both. When Gaby and Eli meet again in the small Texas town they grew up in, one question is uppermost in her mind: is the boy she adored now the man she should fear…or the only man she will ever love?

#1414 MARRIED BY MISTAKE • Abby Gaines
Imagine being jilted on live TV in front of millions of people…. Well, that's not going to happen to this particular bride at Adam's TV station—not if he can help it by stepping into the runaway groom's shoes to save Casey Greene from public humiliation. Besides, it's not as if it's a real wedding. Right?

#1415 THE BABY WAIT • Cynthia Reese
Suddenly a Parent
Sarah Tennyson has it all planned out. In two months she'll travel to China to adopt her beautiful baby girl. But that's before everything goes awry. Apparently what they say is true…life *is* what happens when you're busy making plans.

HSRCNM0307